The Red Island

The Red Island

JIM NELSON

iUniverse, Inc.
New York Bloomington

The Red Island

iUniverse books may be ordered through booksellers or by contacting:

iUniverse
1663 Liberty Drive
Bloomington, IN 47403
www.iuniverse.com
1-800-Authors (1-800-288-4677)

Because of the dynamic nature of the Internet, any Web addresses or links contained in this book may have changed since publication and may no longer be valid. The views expressed in this work are solely those of the author and do not necessarily reflect the views of the publisher, and the publisher hereby disclaims any responsibility for them.

ISBN: 978-1-4502-5557-8 (sc)
ISBN: 978-1-4502-5558-5 (ebook)

Printed in the United States of America

iUniverse rev. date: 9/10/2010

If we could only perform this supreme act of death and restoration every day as well as we had done it the day before, tomorrow and tomorrow as well as last year and the year before, then we would be practically immortal.

Jonathan Weiner

1. Charter Flight

Two men shared exaggerated grins, facing each other in gray leather swivel executive chairs. They were the only occupants of the Gulfstream Aerospace 12-seat cabin. Josiah Crummy lifted a white knight, capturing a black bishop. "Watch out, Casey," he chirped, sipping amber liquid from a crystal brandy snifter. "I've got you on the run."

Casey Robertson laughed, "You haven't beaten me for two years," he boasted. "But I just can't keep my mind on the game. I still can't believe what's happening; we've been snatched from the jaws of doom."

"Pay attention. The jaws of Crummy just captured your knight. Can you believe this plane? These babies cost millions. A few hours ago I kept visualizing me wearing an orange prison uniform, surrounded by nasty brutes needing a shave. Now we're sipping single-malt whiskey and heading for a new life."

"I was almost ready for prison after living in that dump motel with the cockroaches and that obnoxious singing drunk next door. Sorry," Robertson chuckled. "I'm taking your queen."

"Damn and double damn! I don't know why I even bother playing this game. Maybe I just like to hear you say 'checkmate.'"

After months of unrelenting stress, they felt giddy. In a few hours they'd be in South America, living like kings in a country that would never agree to extradition. They had miraculously escaped the long arm of American law. Their suitcases, packed tightly with bundles of $100 bills, guaranteed them a lifetime of comfort and protection. Robertson reached into his pocket pulling out a soiled turquoise plastic disc and a dangling brass key. "Oops," he laughed. "Still got the motel key. Think I'll keep it as a little memento of the Dew Drop Inn."

They had barely eluded converging law enforcement entities. Less than an hour earlier, hiding in a disreputable Seattle motel, they had been startled by thunderous pounding on their flimsy motel room door. Convinced their fugitive days had finally ended, Crummey had opened the door with a sense of deadly resignation. A bulky soldier in desert fatigues barged in and told the men to shut up and listen. Something called "The Chapter" intended to take over their crumbling corporation, despite its pending bankruptcy and criminal lawsuits. A black Lincoln limousine waited outside to take them to Sea Tac Airport where they would board a privately chartered Lear Jet to Bogota...

"In a few minutes the feds will be here. I'm leaving now. Come with me . . . or kiss your sorry asses goodbye."

Hobson's choice. They immediately accepted the offer.

The soldier whisked them to the purring car and clambered in after them. They sat back in the spacious limo speculating on their good fortune in muted tones. The chauffeur was completely hidden behind a black panel of glass. Why would anyone want to take over their company? Who was The Chapter? Why was a soldier helping them? Robinson looked carefully at the uniform for clues—no stenciled name or "U.S. Army" label, no stripes on the shoulder to indicate rank. Even the green beret bore no insignia.

Maybe The Chapter had found a way to produce their drug safely. That had to be it. "Screw the damn drug," Robinson muttered bitterly. They each carried enough money to live like royalty in Columbia. The soldier sat opposite them in uncomfortable, sneering silence. With growing irritation, he had simply ignored their stream of questions.

Half an hour later the limousine hummed through a security gate across the tarmac to the waiting charter. As they boarded, the bulky soldier roughly took the two suitcases. "No luggage in the cabin." He announced. They'll be safe in the cargo hold." Something in the soldier's voice prevented their objection. Mechanically the two men ascended the steps and watched the door glide effortlessly shut. They were greeted by an eager young captain who pointed out the well-stocked bar. He apologized for the absence of a flight attendant. He'd fix meals in the microwave in a couple of hours, with the jet on autopilot.

Moments later, the Crummey and Robertson watched the Lincoln disappear into the early evening dusk. The soldier stretched out his legs in the limo, anxious to know what was so damned important about the heavy suitcases on the seat beside him. Scowling, he unsheathed an ominous black combat knife strapped to his boot, positioning the serrated ceramic blade underneath a flimsy lock. Reluctantly, he changed his mind. How would he explain the broken locks back in Miami?

A small brown spider crabbed across the limousine seat. Clenching his fist, the commando smashed the creature and wiped a streak of tiny organs and tangled legs across the soft leather seat. "Fuckin' spider," he mumbled.

The driver watched Marvin Winter from a small dashboard screen as a hidden camera recorded Winter's every move.

* * *

The young pilot glanced attentively at the amber lights of the cockpit. He had been summoned quickly without the usual complement of co-pilot and flight attendant. Although he had often flown solo, he was going to miss Jackie, his favorite flight attendant, whose stunning good looks, statuesque figure and attentive service invariably coaxed a generous tip from his appreciative passengers. He wondered how important these two bozos must be to afford the $2,000 per hour charter, including the return trip of an empty plane. As he engaged the autopilot, a nearly full moon bathed the snow-capped Colorado Rockies approaching in the distance.

Suddenly, thin streams of acrid yellow-brown smoke began curling from the instrument panel. The pilot smelled burning rubber and sulfur as he slipped an oxygen mask over his face, knocking off his cap. He groped in panic for the radio toggle switch as fingers of smoke began burning his hands and obscuring his mask with an oily film. "Mayday, mayday," he shouted, dismayed at the unprofessional fear in his voice. As the rattled pilot waited anxiously for a response, the sleek jet simply went silent. Both Rolls Royce turbofans had burned out. The plane was now a 35 ton glider, rapidly slowing from its cruising speed of 510 miles an hour. For a precious few seconds the altimeter held steady at 32,000 feet. Then the dial began accelerating counter-clockwise.

The pilot struggled in disbelief to prevent a precipitous nosedive as the cockpit filled with smoke. Terror eroded his professional training as he tried to remember the sequence of actions to re-fire the engines. Then every light on the instrument panel turned black. Why didn't someone respond to his distress signal? He made one last desperate call.

In the cabin, two men stared out the windows in terror as chessmen slid to the plush carpet. Yellow smoke curled silently from the edge of the closed cockpit door. Cabin lights flickered ominously and died, plunging the cabin into darkness.

Robinson clenched the hotel key and mumbled, "Praise God from whom all blessings flow." Crummey jerked his head as sulfurous fumes burned his nose and throat, wailing a hoarse, sickly scream.

2. The Invitation

Tryg Lindstrom opened the refrigerator, shuffling through his gastronomic treasures. Having completed the final sentence of his latest essay "Why is Nature so Cruel?" he was ready for a well-deserved midnight snack. Three jumbo black olives, generous slice of Stilton cheese, dollop of mango chutney, the last bit of hard-smoked salmon—things were looking promising. The small plate was missing something. Aha! Pickled herring in white wine. He impaled the remaining pieces from the jar, extricated them from the fork against the edge of his plate, grabbed a Moose Drool from the bottom shelf and carried the feast in triumph to the kitchen counter where he selected the mini baguette of salt-encrusted French bread. Plunking himself on the living room sofa, plate on the coffee table, he noticed the time: 3:15 am. No wonder he was hungry. He'd been working six straight hours. Thank God tomorrow was Sunday—a day to relax before Monday's two classes and office hours. He had finished his essay a day early and sent it off to *Nature Magazine* with a flourishing tap of a laptop button.

Before sitting down to enjoy his eclectic feast, he gathered his unopened mail from a cluttered desktop. One large burgundy envelope stood out from the rest. Gold gothic lettering on the return address declared "The Chapter." Tryg tore open the envelope and unfolded the gold-embossed card:

* Round trip, first-class ticket to London

* Three-day, four-night stay at the Ritz-Carlton
* Convocation of the premier biologists and biochemists in the world
* Credit card charged with a "conference stipend" of 1,000 British Pounds
* "An extraordinary opportunity to participate in the greatest scientific expedition in history, a one-year sabbatical collecting rare biological specimens"

"Wonder if my passport's current?" he thought.

3.   The Banquet

Dr. Lindstrom, late for the banquet, felt like a teenager at his first prom, dressed in the tuxedo provided by The Chapter. His cummerbund refused to stay in place. Whenever he stood up, he had to readjust it. It reminded him of his first pair of jeans that had insisted on slipping over his narrow teenaged hips. He kept staring at his glossy patent leather shoes; they felt like gaudy slippers with thin leather soles. Even more exasperating, his bow tie had persistently demonstrated "the innate hostility of inanimate things" (a favorite phrase of his best friend and longtime tennis partner). He had spent an agonizing and increasingly exasperating 15 minutes trying to manipulate the band of black silk into a reasonable facsimile of a bow tie. Apparently the familiar pre-tied bow was not *de rigueur* in London. Before braving the discomfort of mixing with a group of strangers, he stopped by the concierge, who deftly corrected the lopsided results of his inept efforts. A quick glance in the hallway mirror marginally boosted his confidence. At least, he thought, he wasn't expected to wear the confounded name badge.

Entering the ballroom, he took in the red mahogany floors, large mirrors in gilded frames, wallpaper featuring unicorns and rampant lions, an army of black-vested waiters and a sea of mauve linen round tables. The sparkling chandeliers echoed light in each mirror and multiplied the apparent size of the room. Tryg, fighting a touch of vertigo, considered bolting when greeted by a "Ritz woman" proffering a manicured, accommodating, tooth-concealing smile. She asked his

7

name and directed him to table 24. Pretty and elegant in a black gown marred only by a gold "Ritz Carlton" badge, his greeter orchestrated her duties with robotic precision, exuding an equally robotic impersonality. Like so many of the Ritz staff, she traded impeccable courtesy, perfect grooming and obsequious service for any hint of genuine personal engagement. Her eyes seemed to look through or beyond him. He consciously turned on his irresistible boyish smile and said, "Thank you." Nothing. Her studied British aplomb had rendered his smile resistible. She reciprocated with the same wide open expressionless eyes (artificial eyelashes, Tryg noted with an unconscious shiver) and frozen smile. The greeter responded, "You're welcome. Glad to be of service, sir," which Tryg took as his dismissal as she effortlessly transferred her attention to the next latecomer.

"She certainly didn't *seem* glad," Tryg thought, smiling unconsciously as his criticism quickly changed to amusement. "She's probably sick of these whining, officious ugly Americans. Before I leave, I'd like to see her drop the mask and laugh or better yet, get ticked off. There's got to be a real person hidden in there someplace beneath the lace-up corset. Maybe even a set of teeth."

As the newest latecomer hurried to her table, Tryg turned back: "Excuse me, ma'am," "may I ask your name?"

"Certainly, sir. It's Allison. How may I help you?"

"Fascinating," Tryg thought. He had expected at least a hint of defensiveness. For a second he was at a loss for words. "Just wondering if my bow tie is straight. I've never had to tie one before."

Allison actually started to smile but those trained lips failed to part. "It's perfect, sir," she responded, recovering her facial neutrality.

Tryg winked and turned back to the meeting. He spied a couple of familiar faces at distant tables, unfortunately already seated with complete parties. Damned if he was going to sit at an assigned place if he could help it. Resigned, he joined nearly 80 fellow scientists in the Marlborough Room. If only he could join Tom Bowman or Jane Oberg, friends and fellow invitees from Harvard. Reaching his assigned seat, he noticed the other five guests engaged in animated conversation, enjoying drinks and appetizers. Tryg made a conscious note to be sociable, or at least not surly. "Evening everyone," he said, feeling a bit warm and hoping his face hadn't changed color. "I'm Dr. Lindstrom," immediately regretting giving his formal title.

A robust man with jet black shiny hair and a prominent purple-veined nose boomed out: "Myron Jacoby. Welcome." Before anyone else could speak, he elected himself social chairman and introduced the others. He was good at names and enjoyed his role. The last to be introduced was Ms. Althen to Tryg's right.

She held out her hand, amending Jacoby's introduction: "Call me Paulette, please." She smiled easily, her deep green eyes locking with his.

"Nice to meet you," he replied awkwardly, sitting down and trying to avert his eyes from an ample bosom. He forced himself to ask Paulette about her academic specialty. He would have preferred asking about her emerald eyes. They were the exact color of a favorite metallic wasp. He nearly began telling Paulette how the wasp preyed on the German cockroach, its grub burrowing inside the victim and eating the organs before pupating inside its dead victim.

Paulette interrupted his reverie by laughing and responding evasively, "I'm a fisher of men, Tryg."

For a second, he had forgotten his question. Before he had a chance to recover from her enigmatic response, one of the ever-present attendants took his order (a Tangueray 10 gin gimlet with crushed ice). Tryg glanced at the banquet menu, deciding on the blue crab cocktail appetizer (narrowly edging out the smoked Scotland trout), Caesar salad, lobster bisque and sirloin medallions. He made a point of rescinding the baby Brussels sprouts. There was an advantage to arriving late. With everyone ordering, imbibing and debating about which of the four forks to use first, he had missed painful minutes of small talk.

He glanced at the two bottles of wine on the table. Few Harvard professors could afford the label Baron Lafitte Rothschild. He had never acquired a taste or appreciation for wine. Instead, he perversely nurtured disdain for pompous wine sniffers. It took considerable effort for Tryg to ignore the comments of the sommelier, extolling the "nose of plum and pepper with a decidedly tobacco finish." Jacoby, however, thoroughly enjoyed the vinophile's ritual, eagerly volunteering to sample the current offering, sniffing the cork, swirling the precious vintage, inserting his ample nose in the goblet, and finally sipping the nectar, eyes closed in mock-erotic reverie. Tryg halfway expected Jacoby to spit the wine into an empty glass. After delaying several seconds for dramatic effect, some of the guests leaning in as if they really cared about his verdict, Jacoby pronounced the wine *maaavelous*. The plump woman next to him actually applauded with rapid little movements of her chubby pink hands. Each of her fingers sparkled with colored stones. With considerable effort, Lindstrom managed to stifle a barrage of sarcastic remarks and a burst of pent-up laughter.

"Wonder if they have any Moose Drool," he thought, glancing at the exit doors where Ms Ritz was escorting an even later arrival to her seat. Everything would have been different, of course, if Tryg's wife had been at his side. She slipped effortlessly into his memory: her contagious laugh and uncanny gift of making everyone feel welcome. At the same time, her firm hand on his thigh would have served as warning him to check his predilection for sarcasm. The crab claw cocktail just made him all the more miserable, recalling those walks along Fisherman's Wharf with his beloved Moira, savoring a slice of sourdough bread and fresh Dungeness crabmeat covered with hot cocktail sauce, served in a paper cup. Even the tenderloin, one of his favorites, did little to lighten his mood.

Moira would have so much enjoyed this trip to London. Without her, the plush accommodations and solicitous service translated into cruel reminders of his loneliness. Eleven years of marriage had ended when Moira collapsed in the kitchen writhing in pain. Two days later, she was dead. The diagnosis was pancreatic cancer. At 38, Tryg had become a widower.

When the Caesar salad arrived, Tryg immediately regretted his choice. The tuxedoed chef arrived with a cart whose silver hood could have concealed a roast bison. His two "helpers" each carried a silver tray crowded with condiments. Creating the hotel's signature salad was a production that indirectly put Tryg uncomfortably in the limelight. The master chef deftly separated an egg yolk in half a shell, cut the anchovies in a blur of swift strokes and grated a snowfall of parmesan cheese. Pickled beets, hard-boiled egg, croutons, bacon bits, oil, vinegar—each joined the unconventional Caesar with enthusiastic tosses. His chubby table mate kept uttering annoying oohs and aahs. Lindstrom tried not to stare at her pink fingers, sparkling with gaudy rings and colored stones.

Finally the attendant deftly placed his masterpiece on Tryg's salad plate and withdrew to appreciative applause, his tall white hat followed by two shorter ones, the trio disappearing like a three-masted schooner.

Sometime between the salad and the tenderloin, Tryg became increasingly aware of Paulette's presence. She wore a fitted emerald green gown that perfectly set off her auburn hair. She was beautiful, he admitted to himself, with classic high cheekbones and perfect teeth. She must be wearing colored contacts, he thought.

Whenever traveling, Tryg and Moira had enjoyed their people-watching game. Women were rated on a scale of 1 to 1,000 ships. Helen of Troy, of course, was the perfect 1,000. Tryg reckoned Paulette would have launched well over 900. He could almost hear Moira describing Paulette in a parody of the Marlowe novels they used to read aloud to each other: "Her legs started at Tuesday morning and didn't end until Wednesday afternoon." Unlike a Sam Spade "skirt," however, Paulette lacked the heavy lipstick and artificial eyelashes. Her natural beauty somehow made Tryg feel all the more uncomfortable.

Waiters hovered, bringing fresh cocktails and deftly popping more corks. Tryg nursed his gin gimlet, relieved to see Paulette temporarily engaged in conversation with the man on her right. But with the next round of drinks, she turned her full attention to Tryg. She didn't seem to fit in with the rest of the guests: Tryg wasn't sure why—too attractive, too young. No, that wasn't it. She was, he guessed diffidently, 30-something. She was too, well, sexy. Even her simple emerald pendant somehow unnerved him. And what did she mean by her "fisher of men" remark? Was she a religious fanatic? Fishing for him? God, was she a hooker? That was stupid—she's an invited guest with an assigned place. Tryg felt himself drifting uncomfortably from *terra firma*. Maybe she's a recruiter for The Chapter, he speculated, wondering why he even cared or, for that matter, why he didn't simply accept her as an academic peer.

He welcomed the distraction of the dessert trolley, filled with artistic *pieces d'resistance*. Curly straws of white and dark chocolate swirled above the éclairs, key lime tequila tarts competed with flourless chocolate cake drenched in amaretto fudge frosting. One offering looked like a miniature sailboat. Tryg opted for a double cappuccino and a chocolate-dipped biscotti. Chubby Fingers and Jacoby ordered raspberries flambé, prelude to another conspicuous production. As the waiter spooned the still flaming raspberries and sauce over dishes of white chocolate ice cream, Paulette turned to Tryg and commented, "Did you ever see a more wonderful dessert?" Something told Tryg she might now be fishing for a compliment; was he supposed to respond that she was far more wonderful or sweet or flaming than any dessert? Was she flirting with him? He hoped not. Moira's death two years ago still felt raw and painful.

He responded with, "Very nice," trying to sound sincere. "How lame," he thought; "now I sound like the Ritz lady. God, I'm such a doofus." He wondered what had happened to his instincts, to the most basic of social skills. When yet another waiter announced final drinks before the presentation, each of the table guests ordered— Drambuie, champagne (Chubby), port, cognac (The Nose). Paulette's order, sparkling water with lemon, intrigued Tryg, content to nurse his cappuccino.

Suddenly Paulette looked directly into his eyes and whispered with some urgency, "We need to talk, Tryg."

"No demure maiden, this," he thought. She was confident and direct. Before he had a chance to stutter an embarrassed response, the lights dimmed.

"Ladies and Gentlemen," the sound system rumbled far too loudly, "President and Chairman of the Board of The Chapter, Benjamin Vaughn St. James." Tryg turned his chair to face the podium.

4.   St. James

Save the Creation. Save all of it! No lesser goal is defensible.
However biodiversity arose, it was not put on this planet to
be erased by any one species. This is not the time, nor will
there ever be a time, when circumstance justifies destroying
Earth's natural heritage.
                                    - Edward O. Wilson, *The Creation*

Only when the chatter stopped did Tryg realize how noisy the Grand
Ballroom had been. People quickly shifted their chairs to face the stage,
although a perimeter of towering screens made the move unnecessary.
As St. James strolled confidently across the stage to the podium,
the academics proffered courteous applause. Known as a ruthless
businessman whose hostile takeovers had consumed dozens of smaller
companies, St. James was feared, hated and grudgingly respected by the
world's power brokers and politicians. But the appearance of one of the
world's wealthiest men was something of a curiosity to this audience.

As St. James walked past the podium, his silver-gray suit, pale
pink shirt, lavender vest and crimson tie lit up six giant screens. Tryg
grimaced at the deeply tanned face and coiffured grey hair. "California,"
he muttered to no one in particular, in obvious disgust.

"Actually," Paulette whispered, leaning forward for Tryg to hear,
"he lives in Miami."

"Even worse," Tryg growled, retrieving his pipe and clamping down
on the well-worn stem.

"Ladies and gentlemen; distinguished guests," St. James began, flashing porcelain-white teeth. "I can't tell you how gratified I am that you have accepted my invitation."

Tryg wondered why he disliked this man so completely and viscerally. He wanted to punch him in the nose, or at least muss up his perfect hair. On second thought, he was loath to touch whatever gel or hairspray held the silver waves in place. "God," he thought to himself, "I hope this is short." He stretched out his long legs and felt his satin cummerbund slide out of place.

"Look around this room and you'll see nearly 80 of the world's greatest biologists. If my count is correct" (confident snow-white-toothy grin indicating he was supremely confident in his numbers), "we have 7 Nobel Laureates, 67 scientists with at least one PhD, and 42 authors of published books. My guests represent 14 nations.

"For the past three years my primary business focus has been on creating the world's most efficient and productive pharmaceutical company. So far no one has taken us very seriously, even though we have built a state-of-the-art laboratory and hired some of the finest biochemists and researchers in the world.

"Let me take a moment to give you a very short overview of the challenges The Chapter faces. For every 10,000 tested molecules of pharmaceutical interest, only one will pass rigorous testing and trials to become an approved medicine. That one drug will take a minimum of seven years to reach public distribution while the others fail at various stages of research and trials. In this high-risk, high-reward industry, the final cost of bringing a single drug to distribution averages $1.5 billion." He paused for a moment to let the mind-numbing math sink in.

Tryg digested the numbers with little real interest, wondering what his colleagues were thinking. Could they possibly care about the economics of the pharmaceutical trade? St. James obviously enjoyed boasting of his power and wealth.

"But the payoff," St. James enthusiastically continued, "is also impressive—projected sales of $1 billion a year for each new successful drug for the life of the patent. In case you're wondering, the typical life of a pharmaceutical patent is 20 years from the time the patent is filed. If a prospective drug actually makes it to the marketplace, 10-12 years typically remain on the patent before the drug goes generic."

Tryg toyed with the idea of slipping away in the relative darkness. He wondered if others felt trapped, as he did, by a sense of obligation to the free trip to London and the expensive banquet. He glanced surreptitiously at Paulette; she seemed to be listening attentively. Jacoby busied himself pouring wine. Nobody was leaving.

"Does the world need another drug company?" St. James continued. There are already about 150 well-established firms like Eli Lilly, Bristol-Meyers Squibb, Merck and Pfizer. Add to these many hundreds of prominent university labs and national institutes, not to mention countless small and boutique companies. In the past decade another group of very specialized competitors has entered the marketplace. These new companies have devoted their resources to bringing biologically promising biota into the laboratory. Drugs from living things—this is the race I'm entering."

Tryg asked himself why he felt so irritated by St. James from his smooth patronizing bass voice to the practiced unrelenting smile and flash of teeth. He was especially repelled by the man's glowing optimism, predicting an obscene profit for his company. Tryg decided on a diversion: he'd count the egotistic presenter's use of first person in his address.

"To date," St. James continued, "three fourths of today's drugs come from rainforest plants. In recent decades ethno-botanists have been living with native peoples, most notably in Amazonia, learning about herbal medicine from the shamans. I have a deep sense of urgency as these tribes and their ecosystems are rapidly disappearing. In the last two years, The Chapter has collected more native medicinal lore than in all other previous efforts combined.

St. James paused, enjoying his own dramatic silence. "Many of you are entomologists. Our focus on insects may seem surprising since the vast majority of pharmaceuticals have been derived from tropical plants. With 7,000 chemistry studies of plants for every one insect chemistry study, plants obviously dominate the field of biological medicines. I am going to change that dynamic. There are possibly as many as 30 million insect species in the world, 100 times that of plant species. I take very seriously the opinion of Thomas Eisner: 'Insects and their relatives are the single most promising and untapped resource in terms of finding new pharmaceuticals from Mother Nature.'"

As St. James continued his sales pitch, Tryg tuned out again, restless and annoyed. He watched the others at his table, their faces bathed in the muted light from the screens. Tryg sampled his cappuccino—lukewarm. Damn! Coffee had to be hot. Disappointed, he put down the cup with a loud click against the saucer. He looked around hopefully, but the wait staff had apparently withdrawn.

"I have exciting news for all of us," St. James continued (milking his audience with another painfully long pause). "Today, I'm announcing the most important biological expedition of all time. The Chapter has committed its vast resources, leveraged with funds from other companies to discover all possible new species on earth. Every year the scientific community adds hundreds of new species. But this process is too slow because every year *thousands* of species disappear forever.

"As E.O. Wilson famously pronounced: 'A rare beetle sitting in an orchid in a remote valley of the Andes might secrete a substance that cures pancreatic cancer.' We want to discover that beetle and find that cure before the beetle disappears.

"With your expert help, we will collect, catalog and analyze a vast new database of earth's biosphere. Your collecting will be focused on new species and particularly on flora and fauna used by indigenous peoples as medicines."

As St. James warmed to his subject, he began to sound more and more like a television evangelist. The choreographed houselights faded until the room was in darkness except for the spotlighted speaker. Tryg sensed, with varying degrees of fascination and discomfort, that St. James was engineering a dramatic finale. Not everyone was so attentive. Jacoby's head had fallen to the side and to Tryg's amusement; the wine connoisseur had begun to snore. The multi-ringed woman next to Jacoby nudged him sharply.

"I come to you today with my promise to the world: nothing less than the complete annihilation of all disease. In this twenty-first century, I hope to see the end of dysentery and malaria, of pneumonia and cancer, of influenza, Alzheimer's, AIDS and the common cold.

"My friends and fellow scientists. . . ."

Tryg groaned out loud. "He's sure as hell not my friend" Tryg thought, "and as far as I know he's not a scientist." Tryg bit harder on the pipe stem and yearned for a fresh, hot cappuccino.

As St. James spoke, the screens flashed color photographs with scientific data.

Agonizing minutes passed as St. James enthusiastically outlined a dozen promising medical discoveries and decried the destruction of tropical rainforests. Tryg's eyes grew heavy as St. James talked about the wonders of the Madagascar periwinkle. After a rich meal and free-flowing wine, many eyes began closing in the warm dark room. Suddenly the house lights reappeared, startling Tryg and most of the somnolent audience.

"Here's the bottom line: I'm asking for your help. Please help me discover and preserve the DNA of countless thousands of species before they're lost forever.

"The Chapter has delivered a contract to each of you, along with the usual Belgian chocolates on your pillow." St. James allowed himself another chuckle. "Please read the simple documents carefully and give me your answer in the next two days. I know that many of you cannot leave your families for a year. Others need assurance that your positions will be waiting for you upon your return. The Chapter will reimburse your universities and labs generously for your sabbatical. I'm confident the financial rewards and unique opportunity we are offering will compensate you handsomely for your sacrifices.

"For those of you willing to participate in this project, I can promise you the adventure of a lifetime. You will live in comfortable, modern modular housing complete with plumbing, electricity, filtered water and plumbing. Each of you has a contract waiting for you in your room, with conditions for your consideration.

"Our mission begins very shortly; for most of you, immediately after Christmas. For now, please enjoy your stay in London. Thank you and good evening."

St. James turned abruptly and left the stage before people had an opportunity to applaud or ask questions. Chairs scraped as everyone rose to their feet and started talking at once. Paulette put her hand on Tryg's arm to get his attention and handed him a business card. She was tall, about 5' 7" Tryg estimated, the top of her head nearly reaching his chin. "I'm in room 1407," she said. "In case you forget, the number's on the back of my card. I'll be expecting you." She wafted out of the room, heads following an outline of curves as she left.

Almost against his will, Tryg admired the receding emerald green figure as he slipped the card and his pipe into his tuxedo pocket.

5. Promises

The London Sun
The end of disease? Yes! promises American tycoon

> *London – Some 80 of the world's prominent scientists met today at London's Ritz-Carlton Hotel to hear American businessman Benjamin S. James promise the end of all disease. "We are rapidly approaching a time when all human disease will be cured or prevented," St. James promised.*
>
> *"My company, The Chapter, leads the world in genetic research and pharmaceutical biochemistry. We are rapidly producing cures for cancer, heart disease, strokes and a host of degenerative diseases. There is no reason, barring injury, why all humans should not enjoy healthy lives for 100, perhaps 120 years.*
>
> *St. James, CEO of The Chapter, is funding a global search for biological specimens that may hold the secret to diseases. "We now have a cure for arthritis," he said. "Dozens of new cures are on the horizon. Living without disease is no longer a dream. It is our future."*

6. The Ritz Club

Curious to see his contract, Tryg decided to return to his room. The Chapter seemed more than willing to throw its money around to "buy" an elite group of scientists. But to him, the location of his assignment outweighed the compensation package. Of all the places in the world, he most wanted to work in an exotic tropical location: Papua New Guinea, Madagascar, Borneo or the Amazon basin. As a kid he had dreamed of catching big bugs in the tropics. Maybe this was his opportunity. He could collect new species for The Chapter and keep an extra copy of showy specimens for himself. As he approached the bank of six elevators, he groaned. A bus of tourists had apparently just arrived, waiting impatiently near a dozen carts piled with luggage and an equal number of porters attempting to marshal their charges. The tourists were now joined by a long line of gowns and tuxedoes from the banquet. "What a bunch of dipsomaniacs we are," he thought, observing that most of his colleagues had brought their drinks with them. Some carried half-full bottles of wine. With an annoyed "damn and double damn" Tryg opted to stroll around the lobby for a few minutes while the congestion subsided.

"Well if it isn't Trygve Shane Lindstrom," boomed a vaguely familiar voice.

Tryg turned around to greet an old college acquaintance, Marvin Winter, accepting the proffered hand and nearly wincing under the aggressive handshake. "What are you doing in London, you old reprobate?" Tryg responded, the chill in his voice conflicting with an involuntary smile. "And wearing one of these monkey suits!"

"You'd better treat me with respect, Doc. I'm a security agent for The Chapter. If you join this great adventure, I'll be keeping an eye on you," Marvin chuckled, but Tryg bristled at the implied threat.

"How did you get into the security business? Last I heard you had left the army and become a French Foreign Legionnaire or something. Come to think of it, I've got a dozen more questions. Maybe you can shed some light on your company. Let's find the Ritz Club. There's a traffic jam at the elevators."

"In London, they call them lifts, old chap," Marvin said in a phony British accent. Tryg declined the requisite appreciative chuckle, refusing to be manipulated. "You look damned good Tryggie. Bet you still play a mean game of tennis."

Tryg winced at the impertinent diminutive, ignored the compliment, if it was one, and sized up Marvin. A star fullback in college, Marvin's physique had become more—Tryg searched for the word—"thick." He was more deep-chested and muscular. The base of his neck was bigger than his head, and his military haircut added to the overall impression of brute power. Marvin was both intimidating and incongruous, muscles bulging uncomfortably inside the tuxedo, stretching creases and straining buttons. Tryg began to recognize other incongruities. Marvin, something of a hot-tempered bully in college, was uncharacteristically deferential and over-eager. Tryg remembered the day Marvin had strutted into the student union with a few of his buddies and challenged any "tennis wimps" to an arm-wrestling match. Marvin had practically pushed one of Tryg's friends out of his chair. "C'mon Tryggie, you chicken?"

As a crowd had gathered, Tryg reluctantly accepted the challenge. Marvin had nearly crushed Tryg's hand before slamming his arm to the table. As the football players left, Marvin had taunted, "You should wear a skirt, Tryggie." The Cro-Magnon's words still carried a sting.

As they walked in silence along the red wool carpet to the west wing of the hotel, Tryg started formulating more questions. They both presented their plastic room-key cards to the uniformed doorman. Tryg froze as he entered the Ritz Club, transfixed at sheer opulence. Marvin ruined the moment by whispering, "Holy shit!"

Tryg surveyed the treasures with a discerning and admiring eye. The walls portrayed idealized youth and beauty in works of Rubens and Gainsborough, Cassat and Monet. Several Greek, roman and art nouveau statues seemed almost to move in the dim light. Then he saw the Vermeer, Moira's favorite artist. He looked at a small bronze plaque: *Young Girl at the Harp, Jan Vermeer, 1664.* He moved to the canvas as if in a trance. As he drew close, he admired the girl, faced away from the viewer, light streaming in the window, illuminating her Titian hair, a grey cat curled at her feet. He couldn't stop staring.

"I wouldn't mind spending a few hours with this little number," Marvin snorted with an evil grin and a voice like crushed gravel, pointing at a young reclining nude. Lindstrom, irritated by the interruption, wasn't familiar with the artist; but the young girl was lovely. He glanced at the plaque: Francois Bouchet, c. 1750.

"Although I've got to say, her boobs are a bit small for my taste."

"You *have* no taste," Tryg retorted, a touch of real disgust in his voice. "Haven't you grown up since college? This place is like a, a museum, a sanctuary to great art."

"Sorry, Doc. Sorry," Marvin stammered, grabbing Tryg's arm. "But the whole damn room is filled with naked bodies," he protested.

Tryg held by the pulsing power of Marvin's thick fingers, jerked his arm away with genuine anger. His questions about The Chapter could wait.

Marvin immediately held up both hands and blurted, "Really, I apologize. No offence, but since when did you get to be so uptight. I was just kidding. I really need to talk to you. Come on. Let's sit down for just a few minutes. Then I'll leave ya alone; I promise."

Reluctantly, feeling trapped yet again by the importunate hulk, Tryg selected a quiet spot with two comfortable flame-stitched chairs. He wanted Marvin to leave so he could admire the room and its collection.

The Ritz Club could comfortably seat 40 people in relative privacy, but so far there were only two other couples. Presumably the other banquet guests were still impatiently scrambling for the next elevator. "Who's that babe?" burst Marvin appreciatively as the mahogany doors opened. It was Paulette, entering alone. She surveyed the room and spotted Lindstrom. Visibly unhappy to see the professor occupied, she turned around and left. "Did you see that piece of prime?" Marvin blurted, abruptly curtailing additional comment lest he offend the overly-sensitive Tryg. "What a stuck-up prig," Marvin thought.

Tryg rolled his eyes and sat down. He'd allow five minutes with this oaf. That's it. Maybe Marvin could give him some inside information on The Chapter. Besides, he admitted to being curious: why was Marvin so eager to talk to him? Almost as soon as they were seated, a waiter appeared in black slacks, black patent leather shoes, a white formal shirt, red silk vest and white gloves. You had to give the Ritz credit for service and style. It was almost spooky how attendants appeared. "How may I serve you gentlemen?" he asked. Tryg was afraid his "gentleman" friend would request the Bouchet woman, with enhanced boobs. Marvin ordered a Budweiser. "Extra cold," he added. "Don't know how you Brits can drink lukewarm beer."

Tryg, mortified at Marvin's incivility, asked for tonic water with a twist of lime. Did the Ritz actually stock Budweiser? he wondered.

As the waiter disappeared, Tryg was taken aback by a look of palpable anxiety on Marvin's face.

7. Marvin's Story

"What's this all about, Marvin. You look as if you've seen a ghost."

"Listen, Tryg. St. James wants me here to convince you to accept his offer. You're one of a few scientists he really needs. He found out we went to the same college together and thinks I can influence your decision. If you don't join this 'great adventure' as he calls it, I'll be looking for a job somewhere else, and I'll never be able to earn the kinda bucks I'm getting here."

"I'll make you a deal, Marvin. You tell me everything you know about St. James, his *Chapter* and this mission of his, and I'll consider joining his merry band. I'm already halfway convinced to tell St. James to go to hell. Something about him just makes my skin crawl. What's his game?"

Tryg began to sense the power he held over Marvin, who was unable to conceal his discomfort. "Wa, what do you mean?" he stammered.

"St. James seems to have all the money in the world. His *Chapter*" (Tryg added a verbal sneer)—"it sounds like some kind of fanatic religious organization—has probably spent half a million dollars just on tonight's little party. Miracle drugs—of course I understand the appeal of that. But why this huge rush? Why are all these scientists setting up shop across the globe in a few *weeks*? It's obvious he's found some very serious investors, and they're expecting a handsome return on their money. But pharmaceutical returns begin years down the road, with all the risk of failure. Tell me now—no BS. Marvin. Tell me what he's up to or. . . ." Tryg hesitated, suddenly knowing exactly what to say. "Or I swear I'm chucking the 'great adventure' and going home on the next plane."

Even in the subdued lights of the room, Marvin visibly blanched. Tryg could understand Marvin wanting to keep his cushy job, but not that unsettling look of fear.

The waiter quietly delivered the drinks and a small box of Belgian chocolates. After the banquet, just looking at the treats made Tryg feel a bit queasy. Marvin drained half his pint glass in a long deep gulp.

"Could I trouble you for a cappuccino?" Tryg asked. "Extra hot," he added.

"Certainly, sir. Anything else?"

"Gimme a scotch on the rocks," Marvin added. "Make it a double." The waiter actually bowed before he retreated.

"O.K., Tryg. Just hear me out. You've *got* to accept your assignment! The Chapter thinks there are maybe a dozen fantastic miracle drugs they can bring to market. I'm talking things like an actual *cure* for cancer. Imagine, a *cure* for diabetes or even AIDS. We've been interviewing tribes in all kinds of remote places like Peru, Brazil, Malaysia, New Guinea, Borneo and the Congo, trying to get secret medicines and herbal remedies from the witch doctors and tribal elders. I've already been on a couple of successful missions. We've been in just about every god-forsaken jungle from Costa Rica to the Amazon and have already brought back dozens of promising plants and bugs, worms and fungus. St. James wants to beat the competition. Lotta companies and universities are combing jungles for miracle cures. St. James is convinced that valuable species are being lost every day and can't stand the thought of a competitor getting to a windfall drug before he does."

"How do you communicate with the native people?" Tryg asked.

Marvin downed the rest of his beer with a deep belch, the pint glass nearly disappearing in his hand. "We travel with a translator, actually an ethno-biologist. He does the talking; I provide the security. In New Guinea we had two security officers in case the cannibals started licking their chops."

Something about Marvin's tone sent a chill up Tryg's spine.

"Some of the stories these natives tell are pretty fantastic," Marvin continued, "like a mushroom that gives you the strength of a hundred men, or a berry that gives you perfect night vision. The U.S. military will pay us millions if we can verify that folk tale and bring back the right berry. I don't know what's so damn important about your assignment, but The Chapter must be after something special, something that's worth a fortune. And St. James wants it *now*. Dozens of new companies are entering the race to discover biological miracle cures. St. James says you're supposed to be an expert on longhorn beetles and wasps, so I'm guessing they're looking for some rare bug. Maybe they've heard stories about an aphrodisiac or a cure for malaria. I'm pretty sure they're going to send you to Madagascar. St. James has sent people there twice to some godforsaken village. We've tried to make friends with the tribe, have given them hundreds of pounds of rice, a couple of dozen arrows, even dug 'em a well. Nothing has worked. They should've sent me. I told St. James I'd get their secret root or bug or whatever—just give me a few minutes with the primitive little buggers and they'd talk."

Again, Tryg recoiled. He had no doubt Marvin wanted to go to Madagascar and prove he could force a tribal leader to reveal sacred lore.

The scotch and cappuccino arrived quietly as Marvin continued. "The Chapter believes you have a better chance of getting information than I do." Marvin didn't attempt to conceal his resentment. "You'll live with the tribe and supposedly earn their trust. Eventually they'll start telling you their little stories. You know, about someone who learned to fly or who turned invisible or who could talk to the animals," he laughed sardonically. "One native in Brazil told us about a mushroom you smoke that turns you into an anaconda for a day. Ninety percent of their stories are pure bullshit or hallucinations. But after a thousand years living in the jungle, I guess they've learned *something*.

"I need to tell you something else, Tryg. I'm married."

"Are you kidding me?" Tryg exclaimed, genuinely surprised and pleased. For a moment he tabled his former–and present—aversion to his erstwhile classmate. "Congratulations."

"Thanks, Tryg. But that's not what I wanted to tell you. Janet, that's my wife." Marvin stopped. His eyes welled with tears and he cleared his throat. "Janet's sick. She's got MS. For some reason, her condition is deteriorating really fast. A year ago, her vision. . . ." Marvin stopped again. He was breathing heavily and cleared his throat. "She's almost blind. Then her legs started to go. I got her a wheelchair. Now she's completely paralyzed from the waist down. The doctors don't know what to do." Marvin bent over, his face buried in his hands. "They think. . . They don't know how long. . . ."

Tryg put his hand on Marvin's shoulder. "Don't say any more. Please."

Marvin quickly composed himself, a bit too quickly for Tryg's sensibilities. "Maybe we can find something to help Janet before it's too late. Why don't you check out your contract to see what little paradise they want you to study? You've *got* to join this mission. If you accept, they've promised me that Janet can be the first one to test any promising medicines."

"Nasty piece of business, that— using your wife as a bargaining chip. I'm beginning to hate this outfit." After an uncomfortable pause, Tryg composed himself. After all, he didn't think he was angry at Marvin, at least not at the moment. "Miracle drugs," he continued. "Makes sense I guess. St. James could care less about vanishing forests. But he cares a lot about any miracle cures he can get before the last trees fall. He's the worst kind of entrepreneur and The Chapter is a greedy, money-grubbing ruthless organization. Maybe no more ruthless than other companies," he conceded. "On the other hand, what if we can cure a few hundred diseases in the next few years? Fact is, if I go, I'll be able to study and collect hundreds of tropical specimens. It's what I've always wanted to do. I don't really care if my discoveries are exploited for profit; they could make the world a better place. You know, the dream of a disease-free world—I actually believe it's possible."

"So you'll go?" Marvin asked, eagerly.

"I'll think about it, Marvin. I really will. And whatever I do, I hope someone can help your wife. Let me find out for sure where they want to send me and how much they're willing to pay. I think it's time to read my contract."

"I've gotta go too," Marvin said, looking at his watch and standing abruptly. He downed the last of his scotch and grabbed the box of chocolates, his right hand squeezed tightly into a fist. A moment later he lumbered through the doors. As relieved as Tryg was to be alone, he found Marvin's sudden departure unnerving. Tryg decided to return to his room to read his contract. Later he could revisit the Ritz Club to spend some time with the priceless paintings and sculptures. But first he needed answers to some nagging questions

1. I know Marvin wants to save Janet. Is that why he looked so terrified?
2. What exactly does the Chapter want me to discover?
3. Who is Paulette and why is she following me?

Tryg drained his steaming cup with appreciation. As he rose to leave the roomful of treasures, he was suddenly jolted by an insight. At the banquet, he had introduced himself as Dr. Lindstrom, but Paulette had called him *Tryg*. He was sure of it.

Paulette Something-or-Other had already known his name.

8. The Contract

Tryg's knees bent slightly as he accelerated upward. Layers of anxiety peeling away as he enjoyed the empty elevator ("Lift," he reminded himself, smiling). First there had been the banquet, with the distasteful St. James and enigmatic Paulette. Then Marvin had imposed himself. He looked forward to the solitude of his room. The lift stopped and Tryg exited, found his room and inserted the electronic plastic key. A corner lamp had been turned on, the bedspread turned down; on his pillow rested burgundy folder and the promised small gold foil box of chocolates.

He picked up the folder, took a seat at the writing desk and clicked on the lamp—nothing. "I bet someone in white gloves will be here in three minutes flat if I call to complain," he chuckled. He was already enjoying the idea of dialing "nil" and pointing out the egregious oversight of a burned-out light bulb. Something about the impeccable service both amused and chilled him. Then he had an idea: the wall switch near the curtains. He flipped the switch and the light responded. Tryg realized he was edgy. He fished his pipe from his tuxedo pocket, nestled it comfortably between his teeth and took a deep breath. That was better. The indented bottom of the pipe stem perfectly matched the point of a lower tooth. He could taste the faint odor of fresh Fjord tobacco in the bowl. Next to the desk, the counter of the wet bar held a tray with a bottle of Tangueray 10 gin, Rose's lime, simple syrup, tonic water, half a dozen wedges of lime and a bucket of ice. "They sure don't miss much," Tryg thought with grudging admiration. At that moment he flashed a mischievous smile his mother would have recognized as a danger sign. Time for a red herring, just for fun. Tryg dialed "0."

"How can we help you, Dr. Lindstrom?"

"Could you send up a bottle of Broker's gin?" he asked.

"Right away, Doctor Lindstrom," came the smooth reply. "Will there be anything else?"

"No thanks," he replied, smiling. Tryg guessed correctly that his personal profile now listed two brands of gin.

He opened the folder, reading each page carefully. Surprisingly, the language was clear and economical, not the legal prolixity he had expected. The Chapter was offering him a twelve-month assignment in the northwest corner of the Malagasy Republic. "Madagascar, Yes!" he exclaimed out loud, raising his fist like Tiger Woods after sinking a 20-foot putt. For a fleeting moment Tryg felt a vague twinge of discomfort remembering that Marvin had mentioned Madagascar.

There was a copy of a letter from St. James. to be sent to Dr. Dupont requesting Tryg's one-year sabbatical. The Chapter would pay Harvard double Tryg's compensation. "I doubt Dupont will need much convincing to get rid of me for a year," he thought. "Or forever." The most attractive concession made by The Chapter: Tryg would be able to keep additional specimens for his personal collection and for Harvard's vast holdings. The Chapter was interested in only one specimen of each new specie.

The page titled "Rationale" especially attracted Lindstrom's attention: three stories. Each documented the exceptional longevity enjoyed by a Malagasy tribal leader or wise man. Each account concerned the same Rock People tribe in northwest Madagascar. The first tale was found in a pirate's journal from the 18th century. The second account, only marginally more reliable in Tryg's opinion, came from a Catholic missionary's diary.

The final entry was contemporary and with some gloss of credibility. A graduate linguistics student, Jennifer Cook, had spent a year in Madagascar collecting folk stories from several Malagasy tribes. According to some of the legends she had collected, a *bibikely* (vague Malagasy term for an insect) sometimes spoke to the wise man or village elder of the Rock People. The *bibikely* had given the elder a magic gift. The insect bit the wise man with what was translated as "the bite that makes the chief live as a young man for 1,000 moons." Although he was the oldest man in the village, he had apparently become a vigorous *tenora lethality* (young man), who had fathered numerous children and lived another 1,000 moons, nearly 78 years by Tryg's literal reckoning, assuming13 full moons a year.

Bingo! Forget the hype about preserving species. What would someone pay for a drug that extended life? Better yet, one that could actually turn back the clock and restore youth? For that matter, barring a terminal disease or fatal accident, why not just live forever? That's just what the world needs—a few thousand really rich people enjoying eternal youth! Just endure the bite of a certain *bibikely*. Around the world, scientists were being recruited to find medicines with staggering commercial value. But the jewel in the crown, apparently, was this quest for immortality. Was that why The Chapter had sent Marvin to recruit him? And Paulette?

Tryg allowed his imagination to stray. How much would someone pay for a sip of the Fountain of Youth? A million dollars to be young and healthy for a thousand moons? How many people would pay a million dollars? Maybe ten thousand people across the globe? That's 10 billion dollars! Tryg shook his head and dismissed the reverie. He just couldn't take the stories any more seriously than Marco Polo's accounts of Madagascar's Roc in carrying off an elephant. Sometimes a legend just a legend. The Chapter may find a cure for Janet's multiple sclerosis, maybe even for pancreatic cancer, he thought bitterly.

The final page was entitled, "Offer of Compensation." Lindstrom had expected something pretty good, but he had to read the number twice for it to sink in: $10,000 U.S. per *month* for 12 months.

$120,000! It dwarfed his current annual salary at Harvard. To Lindstrom, this degree of wealth translated to extended trips to study and collect his beloved wasps and beetles. He took out a piece of Ritz stationery and drew a vertical line down the middle of the page. "A shame to make notes on the gold-embossed linen paper," he thought momentarily. On the left he put a "+" sign; a "-" on the right, and began creating two lists. "Ben Franklin would have approved," he thought.

The + list was easy and forthright, but he was a bit surprised at his negative list. In addition to such concerns as what to do with his house for a year and that he'd miss his friends and colleagues, he listed on-campus baroque concerts, favorite foods, autumn leaves in Cambridge and working with his students. What irritated him most was the distasteful task of collaborating with St. James and his mysterious Chapter to make billions of dollars. His intuition told him there was something sinister about St. James. Of course, if Lindstrom refused to go, another eager and well-qualified naturalist would take his place. Nothing was going to stop The Chapter from hunting for the elusive bug whose "bite makes the chief live many moons."

Tryg crumpled up his list and started over. He asked himself just one question: What is the single best reason to go? The decision was surprisingly easy. He *wanted* to go. He had always wanted to go and that trumped every rationale for refusing. The money would give him financial and, therefore, scientific freedom. Done deal. He'd let The Chapter hire him to hunt for some legendary *bibikely*. Meanwhile, he'd be living his fantasy collecting tropical bugs.

His bottle of Broker's gin arrived just in time to celebrate.

He was going to Madagascar.

Decision made, Tryg pulled off his offending tie. He couldn't believe he was still wearing the thing. He hung his tuxedo jacket over the back of the desk chair. His stiffly starched shirt collar had rubbed uncomfortably all evening. He fumbled through the ruby studs, slipped off his silly patent leather shoes and cummerbund—much better. Flopping down on the massive bed, Tryg surveyed his room. How much fun it would have been to share all this with Moira: the four-poster bed complete with paisley curtains; the hearty British breakfasts, an afternoon pot of tea with biscuits and scones and lemon curd; and most of all, the shower. When traveling, Moira had always insisted on a room with a shower; she would have laughed out loud in joy at this one. The six-by-six room, tiled wall and ceiling in blue-veined white marble, featured two large overhead gold fixtures, the size of dinner plates, issuing a gentle rain. Three separate gold shower heads on the walls encircled the occupants with additional prodigal sprays of warm water.

Suddenly Tryg felt compelled to take a shower. After the St. James speech and the encounter with Marvin, Tryg needed to scrub himself. He slipped out of his clothes and entered the bathroom. The hotel provided an impressive basket of toiletries including such unexpected amenities as a pair of battery-powered toothbrushes. Tryg preferred his own supplies. Still, he rummaged through the basket, selecting the toothbrushes, wondering if they'd be confiscated by airport security. He smiled ruefully at the signature gift: six perfume vials, each a miniature reproduction of the designer bottle, packaged in a small wooden box lined with red velvet. Moira had disdained perfumes. She preferred the simple floral essential oils: lavender, hyacinth, orange blossom and her favorite, gardenia.

The shower took a bit of manipulating: activating all the showerheads involved four faucets, each with its own temperature control and spray volume. As hot water and steam engulfed Tryg, tension drained from his body. He massaged his scalp as the pungent lather of cedar and pine filled the enclosure.

Refreshed, he dried himself with a plush towel and donned the hotel's burgundy velour robe, soft as an alpaca rug. He slipped on the matching slippers.

Surveying the opulence, Tryg suddenly wanted a simpler room in a simpler hotel. No, that wasn't it. He just wanted to go home. There was no reason to stay any longer. He'd leave tomorrow morning, a day early. It felt good to be decisive. He dialed zero and asked for the concierge, who promised to book his return flight.

Tryg returned to his three questions. One should be easy to solve— Paulette! She'd given him her card. Where had he put it? He checked his wallet—nothing. Then he rummaged through his tuxedo pockets— aha! "Paulette Althen." That was it. Just a name. Strange card. No title. No university. On the back she had written simply "Room 1407."

All he had to do was to find her on the roster of attendees with its short bios on each guest. Tryg jumped up and fumbled through the leather book bag he had received at registration, containing the usual welcome letter, a badge to be worn at yesterday evening's "Welcome Cocktail Reception" (the one he had skipped), a three-day Underground pass, an extra room key, a Barclays credit card "loaded" with 1,000 British Pounds, an agenda of events with times and specified attire, the carbonless copy of his tuxedo and shoe sizes for tonight's dinner. There it was! the roster of "distinguished guests." Tryg went over the list twice.

There was no Paulette Althen.

9.   Paulette's Visit

Knock, knock.

"Now what?" Tryg thought. "too late for the maid." He adjusted his robe and opened the door a few inches. "What is it?" he asked.

"It's Paulette," a voice from the hall answered.

Tryg didn't know what to do. What he *did* know was that he had no interest in a casual tryst with the woman, no matter how attractive he found her.

"Let me in, Dr. Lindstrom. Please. It's important."

Tryg tightened his robe and opened the door, surprised to see Paulette in fitted black jeans and a black v-neck cashmere sweater. Without a word she entered the room. Tryg suddenly felt self-conscious—his clothes were scattered on the bed and he was not exactly dressed for company. He noticed the scent of gardenia.

"Sorry for the dramatics," Paulette said, "but this is important. Please, may I sit down and talk?" Without waiting for a response, she took a seat at a round table, making it clear she expected him to join her.

"Like a drink?" Tryg asked. "I've got enough gin for a bathtub and miniature bottles of everything else."

"No thanks," she responded, folding her arms impatiently.

Tryg derived some small satisfaction making his forward visitor wait. The silence was awkward, but he insisted on retrieving a lime wedge and squeezing it over his gimlet. He completed the ritual by opening the Rose's lime and adding a splash. Only then did he sit across the table from her.

"O.K.," Tryg said, betraying some impatience. "Who are you and what do you want? I've already decided to accept The Chapter's offer, so if you're here to convince me, you can leave, mission accomplished. I might as well tell you I've checked the roster of conference members —your name's not listed."

Paulette pulled a small leather wallet from her purse and opened it, revealing an identity card. "I'm Paulette Althen, Special Agent, National Security Agency. I'm here to talk to you about The Chapter."

"Sorry if I was rude," Tryg responded genuinely. "I, well, I just met with one of the Chapter's toadies, an old college acquaintance. He's the one I was with at the Ritz Club. He's been pressuring me into accepting The Chapter's offer. And then you've been trying to see me—thought you two were playing good cop, bad cop. At least I figured you for the good cop," he said, flashing his best schoolboy grin. "You know how paranoid we entomologists can be. My alternate theory was, well, that you were, flirting with me," he chuckled a bit uncomfortably. "Been single for a couple of years. Don't know the signs any more. Maybe I just wanted to believe a beautiful woman—sorry, can we start over. I'm feeling stupider by the minute. I can't seem to stop talking. Guess you're here to put me under arrest?"

"I seem to have forgotten my handcuffs," she smiled. "How about you relax and give me a few minutes of your time, Professor. If you want, maybe I could arrest you tomorrow."

"O.K., O.K., *Special Agent Althen*," Tryg capitulated, punctuating the words gently and stifling a grin as he held up his hands in surrender. "I'm listening."

"St. James is already uncomfortable that I'm here; he thinks I'm with the Food and Drug Administration and reluctantly agreed to let us monitor his conference since someone in the Pentagon had quietly approved a nifty multi-million dollar grant for this grand venture.

"For some reason, you seem to be one of the golden-haired boys in this project. Two of St. James' investors have threatened to leave if you don't accept your assignment. We've already completed a complete background check on you, Professor. We know you're something of a wiseass and a popular teacher. You've got a masters degree in English literature and a PhD in entomology, drive a 10-year-old Honda, listen to baroque music and like to fly fish in Montana. You're a liberal, a

Democrat, a mediocre guitar player and you still keep a picture of your late wife on your bedside table. You had a wisdom tooth pulled last year, seem to be addicted to cappuccino, and you've got asthma. You're latest book is practically a best seller. You've got thirty pairs of identical black socks but a variety of colored briefs, and not a single pair of boxer shorts. Should I go on?" Paulette smiled demurely.

"You didn't mention my stamp collection," he quipped lamely, wishing he had delivered a more clever repartee. "No wonder you called me Tryg at the banquet."

"I hoped you hadn't noticed that unfortunate slip," Paulette smiled. She retrieved a Blackberry from her purse and scrolled through the text. "Says here you specialize in North Borneo, the Australian states and Papua New Guinea lakatois. What the heck's a lakatoi?"

Tryg was impressed. "Does it mention I use Arm and Hammer toothpaste? Never mind, I don't want to know. A lakatoi's a kind of native canoe with sails. I'll probably regret this next question, but what do you want me to do?"

"Unlike St. James, I'll be brief," Paulette said. "For the past three years several government agencies have been watching The Chapter with growing concern. St. James has accumulated enormous resources, more than $10 billion, some from very questionable alliances, including organized crime. That got the FBI and DEA interested. Suspicious deaths in Congo and Peru may be linked with The Chapter, attracting the CIA, Interpol, and other international law enforcement agencies. The Chapter's focus on biological toxins has caught the attention of the FDA and a division of Homeland Security specializing in biological warfare. Meanwhile, some three-star general in the Pentagon is hoping for biochemical enhancements for his infantry troops—anything from extraordinary stamina to night vision. Recently, Admiral Tatum, the redoubtable Director of the National Security Agency, assigned me fulltime to researching The Chapter. Essentially we're a communications intelligence agency; we've started monitoring all Chapter communications. Unfortunately, they use state-of-art secure encryption technology. To use NSA terminology, we're 'deaf.'

"Remember a company called Natural Cures from the Amazon?"

"I think so," Tryg replied. "Didn't it just go through bankruptcy?"

"The very same," Paulette said. "It was the creation of two insect collectors, Crummey and Robertson. They made a fortune on a bombardier beetle from Brazil. Gives me the creeps; looks kind of like a black widow spider. And those jaws, ugh! Anyway, the natives told these two collectors about how munching on this beetle takes away pain in their joints.

"Well, C and R, had been spending their time in places like Africa and Brazil and Indonesia buying insects for collectors. They pay the natives a few cents for each specimen and then return to their warehouse in Texas with hundreds of delightful dead crawlies for auction on E-Bay.

"Of course, they're always looking for the gems, really rare bugs— whatever collectors will pay a bunch of money for. They recently sold an eight-inch *Titanus* something-or-other for $10,000 to a Japanese collector. Ugly brown thing looks like a cockroach. Apparently they have no scruples when it comes to bending the law. Somehow they've managed to smuggle a steady stream of protected rare species without CITES permits. Seems there are plenty of buyers who will pay to have illegal insects in their private collections."

Tryg was growing more furious by the second, hating poachers who would gladly kill a rhino just to remove its horn, or a snow leopard for its exquisite fur. CITES protected all kinds of animals, even rare insects. He'd love to put Messers C and R behind bars.

Paulette continued. "So these two are in Brazil, collecting rare bugs and they make friends with a shaman who tells them about this amazing beetle. Pick it up and you'll be sorry. It sprays something like ammonia and pepper spray—and it's hot! I mean nearly boiling. But there's some other chemical in the beetle that really *is* a miracle drug. It not only takes away the pain of arthritis—it seems to cure it!

"So C and R take home a couple of dozen dead bombardier beetles and open up C and R Natural Cures from the Amazon. Forget buying and selling bugs. They're after the *big* money. They dry the beetles, grind 'em into powder, dilute it with 1000 parts cornmeal or flour or something and create. Herbs and natural products aren't regulated by the FDA. They start selling this miracle arthritis cure for $99 a pill, claiming it's some kind of tropical herb. One pill a week for six weeks is apparently all you need; they even offer a money-back guarantee. They get some testimonials and start running an ad on late-night television. Guess what? Orders start pouring in. Better yet, their concoction actually works. People swear the pain of arthritis disappears in hours. And after a couple of weeks, the effects of arthritis may actually begin to reverse. You should see the "before and after" pictures. People with swollen knuckles look normal after a month. In three months, C & R sold some 60,000 of their little pink capsules at $99 apiece plus $14.95 shipping and handling. They split a nifty million dollars profit.

"Over the next year they managed to purchase more beetles, diluting the mixture even more and pocketing millions. They even had an invitation to appear on Oprah!"

"Unfortunately for C and R, there was a serpent in their little paradise. It seems that a bunch of stuff in the beetle powder was dangerous, even carcinogenic. Instead of isolating the chemical that actually cures arthritis, they just used the entire beetle. A few people developed disfiguring cancers. Several have died.

"C and R were stupid and greedy. They kept buying beetles and selling their miracle drug, even as the reports of cancers and deaths accelerated. They swore that an independent lab had tested the beetles and that the pills were safe. Some victims developed terrible, fatal bone cancers where the arthritis had been. Pretty soon attorneys and process servers began knocking on the doors of C's mansion and R's summer home in the Bahamas. Their famous pink capsules disappeared from the shelves. Natural Cures from the Amazon folded its tents. But people were still dying painful deaths. Facing criminal charges, subpoenas and depositions, C and R emptied their bank accounts and ran. We traced them to Seattle; suddenly they've disappeared.

"But here's the kicker. Guess who isolated the formula for the active and completely safe ingredient that cures arthritis?"

Lindstrom already knew the answer. The Chapter's Cray computers and biochemistry labs had isolated and patented the active molecule. Hadn't St. James announced that The Chapter was already marketing a safe cure for arthritis?

"Now they're after you. The Chapter thinks the natives in Madagascar know something. They're expecting you to send them a miracle bug. We've read The Chapter's proposal to you. They want nothing less than the fountain of youth.

"All we really have so far is a lot of circumstantial evidence that's starting to add up to an ugly picture. We suspect The Chapter of widespread criminal activity; apparently the company knows few ethical boundaries. We want you to keep your eyes open and be careful. Assume everything on your computer and all your e-mails are being monitored by The Chapter. Assume they've tapped into your home phone, cell phone and office phone at Harvard. St. James is a ruthless SOB. He's taken over a dozen companies and destroyed as many others. His entry into the medical arena intrigues a number of federal agencies, from FDA to the IRS. It usually takes years for a company to start turning a profit; we know The Chapter's investors are demanding a fast and handsome return on their money. The stakes are high. St. James will stop at nothing to crush his competitors and generate an even greater personal fortune. I can't prove a thing, Tryg, but if you discover anything illegal, even suspicious, please contact me.

"The Chapter has provided each participating scientist with an amazing laptop. It weighs over 12 pounds, but should survive pretty much any ordeal. The case is dustproof and waterproof. It has proprietary software that connects to the Internet by satellite; and you'll be able to communicate from pretty much anywhere except maybe inside a cave or a bank vault. Supposedly the machine will survive a drop of six feet onto a sidewalk. Here's the kicker. Each of these computers is connected to the Chapter's mainframe. They'll be reading every word you enter and every e-mail you send."

Paulette reached in her purse again and produced a thin silver card. "This is our ace in the hole. The NSA calls it a *switcher*. Plug it into the computer and your screen will turn dark for a couple of seconds. The Chapter will think you've just shut down. In actuality, you've switched the computer over to us. Your screen will open again with a small icon of a bumble bee—nice touch, eh? Picked it out myself, just for you, Tryg. Click the icon and you're on a secure e-mail that will be sent directly to me at Fort Meade. Anything I write to you can be transmitted to you only when the switcher is activated, so you need to use this little device every day you're in Madagascar. And please don't lose it—it cost Uncle Sam more than four years of my salary. For extra security, the switcher is also a scrambler and descrambler. If anyone figured out a way to intercept a transmission while you're using the switcher, all they'd get is thousands of random characters."

"What other scientists are working with you?" Tryg asked.

"You're it, Professor. We're looking into The Chapter's other top priority assignments, but we haven't finished our security background checks. So for now, all my eggs are in the Lindstrom basket."

"Paulette?"

"Yes?"

"Isn't this where you show me my cool spy weapons? Sorry for the cold reception when you first got here. We better be friends."

"It's about time! After all, I know about your underwear and lakatois. Generally I call a man by his first name *way* before I know about his underwear. Agreed—friends?"

Tryg reached across the table and shook her hand. "Only seems fair that I get to look at your toothpaste and underwear first. But I guess the bumblebee icon more than makes up for that. Friends. How about that drink?"

"Got any more tonic?"

While Tryg got up to pour the tonic, she continued, "At the moment we have nothing to pin on St. James. He's a powerful man with powerful friends. The Director has made it abundantly clear that we proceed with utmost caution before we, quote, 'Nail his sorry ass.' The Director's convinced St. James is a nasty character, and he's totally committed to bringing The Chapter down.

"If you agree to work with us, with me, you'll need to sign some documents. In essence you'll become a federal subcontractor, subject to half a dozen national security statutes. You already have a Top Secret Crypto security clearance, required to use a switcher and to open your bumblebee. Oh yeah; I almost forgot. You'll be working for Uncle Sam, *gratis*. I'm hoping it's an offer you can't refuse. So, will you help us?"

"It's so hard to say 'no' to such a beautiful spy. Besides, I already think St. James is a creep. Count me in. Do I get an undercover name and a decoder ring? And don't forget the pen that doubles as a flamethrower." Paulette rolled her eyes and handed him a stack of papers stamped with various caveats: *Top Secret, Cryptography Clearance, National Security Agency, By Authority of the President of the United States.* He signed each one with aplomb, not bothering to read the pages. "In for a penny," he said. "By the way, are your eyes really that green or are you wearing contacts?"

"Thanks for your cooperation, Tryg," she said, gathering the papers and checking each signature line. "No contact lenses. I do eat a lot of spinach though. One last thing, Tryg"

"What is it, oh spy leader?"

"Maybe I *was* flirting with you. . . a bit." She smiled and stood to leave, her deep green eyes locking on his. Then she was gone.

"I think my guitar playing is better than *mediocre*," he grumbled.

10. Thieves in the Night

London Times
Biological Research Labs Burglarized

In the past week, two high-security insect bio-research facilities have been burglarized. Australia's CSIRO (the Commonwealth Scientific and Industrial Research Organization) announced recently that the high-security bio-research facility Entocosm was ransacked with the loss of undisclosed materials. Entocosm has produced a number of insect enzymes and proteins of commercial value. A defensive chemical from the Australian cathedral termite, for example, has powerful antibiotic properties. Entocosm has also published research on promising insect proteins that destroy selected microbes, including pneumonia-causing bacteria.

Most intriguing, however, is the rumor of a family of insect-based molecules that seek out cancer cells without harming surrounding healthy tissue. Could this research lead to the next blockbuster drug? Entocosm publicity director Ian Graham has declined to comment.

A second break-in was recently reported at the French company, Entomed, headquartered in Strasbourg. Highly-

*skilled thieves foiled the facility's security system and stole
an undetermined number of cultures of unique bacteria
found on insects. Entomed is the first laboratory to have
successfully culture these insect bacteria in a laboratory.*

11. The Tutor Arrives

Tryg answered a series of dull thuds on the door. No metallic clang of the prominent gryphon doorknocker; no doorbell chorus of "It's a Small World After All." (Moira had it installed years ago honoring Tryg's promotion to full professor.) His expected guest was definitely thudding. Lindstrom opened the door and burst into laughter at the large humanoid shape, bundled in a snow-white arctic parka complete with fur hood, oversized mittens, ski pants and winter boots. The face—assuming the figure *had* a face—was barricaded underneath a black high-altitude ski mask complete with breathing filter and built-in goggles. Granted, it was a cold evening with large snowflakes swirling in the air, but this visitor was outfitted for a polar winter.

"Dr. Lindstrom, I presume?" came the muffled voice, from the figure towering over Tryg by several inches and extending an enormous mittened hand.

"Nice to meet you, Dr. Oten—if you *are* Dr. Oten," Tryg chuckled. "Come on in out of the cold."

"Please drop the formalities, professor," the muffled voice continued as the figure stepped across the threshold. He slipped down his hood and removed the mask. "My friends call me Mamba. It means 'crocodile' in Malagasy."

"And you can call me Tryg. Welcome."

The visitor stamped a bit of offending snow from his boots and entered the professor's home, taking off a mound of brand-new winter wear, starting with the mittens. Tryg held out his arms to gather a succession of wool, Gore-Tex and goose down. Tryg noted Mamba's handsome black face and natural grin. With some difficulty, Tryg gathered up the knee-length coat, mask, scarlet scarf and mittens, dumping them in a heap on the guestroom bed. Mamba was still wearing bib-overall ski pants, a turtleneck sweater and Caribou boots. Tryg immediately liked his guest, from beaming smile to intelligent eyes.

"Welcome, my friend, I've been expecting you. What do you do when you're not braving blizzards to tutor foolhardy bug men?"

"Same as you, Professor. I play with six-legged critters. Mamba Oten at your service," he continued with a short bow. "I'm a big fan of yours."

"Oten? Oh . . . my . . . God! You're the weevil king! I didn't make the connection. You just discovered the totally red variety of *Tracelophorus giraffa*! I've got the article right over there," he exclaimed, pointing to a massive oak desk piled with a precariously balanced mountain of papers, journals and books. "Professor Oten, the honor is mine! But I thought you were teaching at Oxford."

"I'm on sabbatical. Moved back to Madagascar six months ago— not sure I'll ever return to London. Winters there are almost as cold as in Boston! St. James invited me to join the merry band of men and women at the Ritz in London, but I've got a wife and son and another child on the way. We've all come home to Tana to have our baby and re-introduce little Mamba to his doting grandparents.

"I met St. James in Tana a few weeks ago. Tana, that's what most of us call Antananarivo, the capitol. He kept pestering me with questions about the Rock People. I didn't especially appreciate the inquisition. Besides, what makes *me* an expert? I've only visited them once. Did St. James expect them to tell me some fabulous secret? Finally, he made me an offer—come to London for some conference. No offense, Professor, but I think he wanted *me* to work with the Rock People. After all, I know the language . . . and the fauna."

"St. James was in Madagascar? That pompous ass! Oops—I better show a bit more respect. Guess he's my boss now."

"Now he has to pay both of us. I'm getting an obscene amount of money to teach you for a few days and then to identify the bugs you find on your safari. I won't be much help on spiders—just send 'em all to

The Chapter. St. James seems damned eager for you to find a particular bug; my guess is it's a longhorn."

"What makes you think I'm looking for a longhorn, Mamba?"

"You're going to spend the whole year with the Rock People. When I visited their tribe, I went to their burial grounds. You can tell a lot from a Malagasy burial ground, me boy. Look at the gravesite carvings. You'll see a lot of very graphic sex: people and animals or birds co-mingling, displaying remarkably disproportional sexual appendages. But at the very top of each totem, most Malagasy tribes display zebu horns. The Rock People substitute a longhorn beetle. For some reason, going back centuries, the beetle is sacred to them."

Tryg looked thoughtful but remained silent.

"But I don't think St. James has any idea what he's looking for. Everyone here has heard stories of the Rock People, but they're vague. We Malagasy don't even have a word for 'longhorn' or 'beetle' for that matter. And no tribe is as secretive as the Rock People. Glad to see you're not a clone of St. Pompous-Ass James. Shouldn't have worried. To misquote Will Rogers, 'I never met an entomologist I didn't like.' We'll make a great team—you collect 'em and I'll get the curator of invertebrates at the Madagascar National Museum of Nature and Science to identify them. I just happen to be best friends with him."

"Who is he?"

Oten flashed a silly grin, pointing to himself and hooking his thumbs under his overall straps.

"Mamba, you are indeed a treasure chest of surprises!"

"I maintain the definitive catalog of insects in Madagascar (*Madagasikara* in our language). I'm looking forward to adding hundreds, maybe thousands of new species to our museum and (with a little luck and cajoling) special requests to my personal collection. You'll find all kinds of wonderful things. I'll be expecting you to keep your eyes peeled especially for lovely new weevils and metallic beetles for my collection. I'll be your taxonomist; just send me digital photos every once in awhile, and I'll do my best. I'll send you digital photos of our collection too, so you can eliminate as much duplication as possible. With some luck, you'll discover lots of new species every week."

"Do you really think I'll find so many?" Tryg asked incredulously. "Hundreds of scientists have studied Madagascar for the past few decades."

"How true," Mamba laughed. "We're practically overrun with naturalists and students. Not to mention the busloads of tourists looking for lemurs. But they've barely scratched the surface of our biota. Do you know where Madagascar ranks in hotspots? We're number one by a huge margin with nearly 500 genera of plants and mammals. No one knows how many unique genera of invertebrates. A couple of years ago they found a supposedly unknown 65-foot palm tree for God's sake. It's right in your neck of the woods, by the way. Last year they found two new species of lemurs, three new birds and nearly a dozen new frogs. There are probably a million new bugs to find in *Madagasikara* alone, me boy. Most scientists study our lemurs or other unique mammals, the aye-aye of course, the amazing chameleons, birds and orchids, but the invertebrate population is largely undiscovered and ignored.

"Oh by the way, here's a little gift for you," Mamba said, patting a lump on the side of his snow pants.

Pulling a small cardboard box from a pocket, he handed it to Tryg, who lifted two metal clasps to remove the cover, revealing a smaller one. He was very familiar with the special packaging entomologists used to ship specimens. He had sent and received hundreds of insects in the same double-boxed format. Sure enough, inside the second box was a two-inch insect case with a single pinned beetle—a pure red giraffe beetle labeled *Tracelophorus giraffe* var. *mamba*.

Tryg was speechless. He just stared at the rarity, a two-centimeter-long, giraffe-necked weevil, the very one pictured in the *Nature* magazine on his desk.

Before Tryg could manage to speak, Mamba interrupted. "This is the second specimen I've found—both males. I have one and now you have the other, but keep it quiet. St. James has been pressuring me to send it to them; they want to test anything with bright warning coloration. They crush each specimen into powder and then run their tests. All they want is the molecular chemistry. No way I'm giving this gem to them. They can wait until I find a few more; next one goes to our national museum."

Whenever Oten laughed or flashed another boyish grin, Tryg found himself grinning in return. "Tell you what, Mamba, when I find a new species—a particular beauty, it'll bear the honored name, *otensei.*"

Little did either realize the consequences of that innocent promise.

12. Orientation

Andrianampoinimerinand riantsimitoviaminandriampanjanjaka
(name of the King of Madagascar, 1787-1810)

Tryg led his guest to a small living room faintly scented with pine smoke. Books lined two walls, floor to ceiling. A huge oak desk with three rows of short drawers ascending nearly to the ceiling, dominated one corner. Its six-by-four foot desktop was a cacophony of books and papers crowding a laptop computer. The fireplace glowed with the remnants of a Yule log. Mamba didn't see a stereo, but heard a Baroque string quartet, Corelli or Telemann, he guessed. He stopped at the upright Schimmel, admiring the deep mahogany color and the glass-like surface. Above the piano was a red lacquer display case filled with beetles. One was turquoise, another bright yellow, a third deep green with grey spots. A fourth was covered with burgundy velvet "fur" and displayed with fearsome open jaws. All were impressive, three to four inches long with antennae longer than their bodies. But the centerpiece was a silver specimen with 10-inch-long antennae curving around the sides of the case. Next to the piano stood a Victorian cabinet of curiosities.

"Join me for a drink?" Tryg asked.

"Thanks," Mamba answered simply, absorbed in the eclectic collection of artifacts in the cabinet.

"Let's see." Tryg opened a door above the kitchen counter. "I've got Armagnac, gin, tequila and Moose Drool beer."

"You pulling my leg, Doc?" Mamba laughed. "Moose Drool?"

"It's a microbrew from Montana, the state where I grew up. You'd love it there—almost cold enough for your North Pole suit and lots more snow than we have here. I try to contribute to my home state economy whenever I have a chance. They feature Sam Adams on tap at the Harvard Student Union pub, but whenever I have a few grad students over, we break out the Moose Drool. Like to try it?"

"Tempting," Mamba laughed again. "But in this blizzard," he said, shivering and glancing at the coals, "I'd go for the Armagnac."

"Be right back." Tryg, announced, walking to his kitchen bar. "Make yourself comfortable. You could even take off your ski pants," he added, laughing.

Mamba wasn't about to abandon any more layers of clothing prematurely. He moved his face close to the display case for a closer look. The top shelf held an antique brass microscope and a three-inch long skull of a Gabon viper with large curved fangs. Somehow the delicate skull looked more even more ominous than the living snake. The next shelf held seashells—a Venus comb, a large bright yellow cowry, several cone shells—and a seven-inch-long fossilized Megaladon tooth. The third was a rainbow of colored crystals, amethyst, tourmaline, rhodochrosite, citrine, pink calcite, and fluorite. He had to kneel to look at the bottom shelf featuring several opals in matrix, something brown the shape of a football—Mamba guessed it might be an unusual wasp nest—and a silver-bladed fishhook.

Tryg returned with the Armagnac in a brandy snifter and a tall glass with what Mamba correctly guessed was a gin and tonic with a wedge of lime and ice cubes. "Cheers"

"Red mud gets in your blood," he returned.

"Haven't heard that one before," Tryg laughed.

"It means, well, with all her faults, *Madagasikara* and her red soil grows on ya. You'll see. Just when you're ready to leave the damn mosquitoes or the government bureaucracy behind, you realize you love the place and the people, especially the people. Or maybe it just means that the mud really does get in your blood," he said grinning, savoring the Armagnac. "You might as well get used to it. The soil is red. The rivers run red when it rains; the island is ringed by red silt merging into the ocean. We often say our island is bleeding to death. Lot of truth to that, Tryg," he added sadly. "Your clothes gradually get stained with it.

Don't be alarmed when you sneeze—even your mucus is red as blood. The whole island is a huge deposit of red laterite. But to change the subject, it appears I've stumbled upon the lair of a mad scientist. Gabon viper skull, tarantula fangs, spider in amber, mud dauber nest . . . you could start your own museum."

"Sorry, Mamba; I'm not much of a host. Make yourself comfortable by the fire," Tryg said, motioning to the two flame-stitched, wing-back armchairs facing the fireplace.

Mamba sat down and held his palms toward the fire screen, gratefully soaking up the heat.

"How about we stoke up the fire?" Tryg said. "I don't think you've thawed out yet!" Tryg, dressed in a polo shirt, herringbone tweed jacket and khakis, couldn't help chuckling again. "I think you've been in the tropics too long; a fire, and the Armagnac, should warm you up." He laid two split logs on the coals. "So how'd you get the name 'crocodile'? Born with teeth?"

"My dad believes the name will protect me from a crocodile attack. So far it's worked," he grinned. "Most of us have our French or English names as well as our spiritual tribal names. My kid brother is 'Biby' and my sister is 'Fanenitra;' they mean 'beast' and 'wasp.' I like to tell them that instead of protecting them, they turned into their names!"

"Bet you're exhausted. How was your trip?"

Mamba made no attempt to conceal his delight as a shower of sparks raced up the chimney and flames began lapping the new supply of wood. "The trip's pretty brutal, as you'll soon find out. With all the stops it took 39 hours. I still haven't changed to Boston time. Had to get a newspaper to be sure what day it was! But I slept like a *maty lehilahy,* a dead man most of yesterday." He took an appreciative sip of the Armagnac and began to relax.

"How's your hotel?"

"It's amazing. Have a Jacuzzi in my room! Wish I had come with my wife and kids. Buffet breakfast! Little refrigerator filled with tempting libations—a cold Heineken's a mere ten bucks and a bottle of water costs only five," he laughed. "Let me read this to you. It's priceless." With some difficulty he reached inside his ski pants and pulled out a small card. *To our valued patrons. This bottle of artesian spring water is provided for your convenience. Should you choose to consume it, your room* *will be charged $5.* I guess the hotel needs the money. My room costs a mere $349 a night, plus about $50 in taxes. Good thing I don't have a car—parking is another $40 a day—for the *convenience of patrons* no doubt. Oh yeah, Internet service is $15 a day. Sure glad St. James is paying the bill!

"When I looked out my window this morning, I knew I was in trouble. Snow! And all I had to wear was my tropic fatigues—and a raincoat. The concierge took pity on me. Next thing I knew I was sitting in the back of a hotel limo on the way to an outrageously expensive sporting goods store. What do you think of my winter wear?"

Tryg laughed again. "I wouldn't mind having that stuff for ice fishing my dad and I used to do on the Kootenai in Montana, or maybe next time I visit the Antarctic."

"Never should have asked a Swede," Mamba grumbled. "Bet you were born in an igloo!"

"Watch it! I'm Norwegian. It's true that we nurse on icicles," Tryg bantered. "But only Swedes, North Dakotans and a few hardy Eskimos live in igloos."

The fire was now crackling noisily. "You know what, I can't believe it but I'm actually getting warm. Think I will take off the ski pants." Mamba struggled to slip off his boots, revealing heavy gray wool socks with a red stripe near the toes. "Check these out," he said, slipping out of the ski pants and pointing proudly to his new jeans. "They're lined with flannel." Mamba walked into the guest bedroom and tossed the ski pants on the mound of his other clothes, setting the boots at the foot of the bed.

"Welcome to the Boston Blizzard," Tryg said, reaching for the Armagnac bottle and refreshing his guest's empty snifter.

"I was looking at your display cabinet. I presume there's a story behind the fishhook?"

"You know, you're the first one who's ever asked about it. I grew up in a little town called Libby. It's beautiful country, with dozens of lakes and streams and rivers. The Kootenai runs right through it. Used to be a big lumber and mining town. Now it's, well," Tryg hesitated, his voice softened, "quieter. Anyway, one day my dad took me fishing on Libby Creek, about 12 miles from town. I was seven. Had all my own stuff—wicker creel, bamboo fishing rod, even a fishing vest several sizes too large for me. Had a brand new Bob Bet Bait Box on my belt, filled with a dozen night crawlers Dad and I had dug up. Dad walked downstream a hundred feet so, pretending not to watch me. I insisted on fishing by myself, like a man," Tryg laughed.

"Well, I managed to string the pole and tie on a hook—this very one, a number 4 Eagle Claw spinner. Can't find ones like these any more with the little dark red beads. Somehow I managed to impale a night crawler on the three hooks. I put on a couple of lead shot and cast into the deep pool dad had picked out for me. Bam! First cast! A rainbow grabbed the worm and I jerked the pole with all my might. Good thing Dad had tied on a 12-pound test line! The fish came flying out of the water like a rocket and I fell over backwards. It landed beside me, flopping on the rocks. I picked up the fish with both hands, yelling like a banshee for Dad to come see.

"Of course he had seen the whole thing. It was my first real fish, you know, all on my own. Eighteen inches! That night I fed our family with my trout. As they say in Montana, a vegetarian is just a lousy fisherman. Never used that spinner again—didn't want to take a chance of losing it."

Studying a display case on the wall, Mamba commented, "You've got some really nice beetles, Tryg. I'd sell the family zebu for that Batocera—antennae must be 25 cm long! And that horseshoe crab on the wall—it's a foot and a half across!"

"Found it myself on the beach," Tryg said with ill-concealed pride. I've got a collection of 'em from an inch long to this monster. They look just like fossils that are millions of years old. They wash up on the east coast beaches. I'll send you a few. And consider the Batocera yours. It's the least I can do. I have a friend in Papua New Guinea who will send me another. So your family raises zebu?"

"Yep, they're all over Madagascar. You'll see a small herd of 'em with the Rock People. Look a little like your Texas longhorns."

"Warm enough for you now? Tryg asked as the fire crackled merrily. "You'd think you were from someplace like Africa! Make yourself comfortable while I make us a couple of ham sandwiches before we get down to business."

"Thanks, Tryg. Mind if I snoop around the Lindstrom museum?"

"Snoop away," Tryg called from the kitchen. "Coffee or tea, or just more Armagnac?"

"Coffee, thanks."

A bit reluctantly, Mamba left the crackling fireplace and padded in his socks to the massive oak desk. He counted the drawers that rose above the desk: three columns of nine, each with a brass handle and brass labels. He opened a drawer marked "Lucanidae" and gasped: four rows of monster fearsome-jawed stag beetles, perhaps 40 species in all. He glanced over the labels until he spotted three drawers labeled *Curculionidae*: weevils! The first drawer held green, gold and turquoise gems from New Guinea. In the second he found a pair of giraffe beetles. "Hey, Tryg. You didn't leave room for your Mamba variety of *T. giraffa*."

"That one goes in my cabinet," Tryg called, "with my special treasures." Tryg entered with four enormous sandwiches and two steaming mugs of coffee. He set the tray on a small table between the two comfortable chairs that faced the fireplace. "Ham and cheese sandwiches and a couple of cappuccinos. Now we're living!"

As they gamely attacked their second sandwiches and Tryg refilled their mugs, he said, "OK, um, Crocodile, what are you here to teach me?"

"It's 'Mamba'—and I don't really know why I'm here. The Chapter offered me $5,000 plus expenses to come to Cambridge for a week. I'm going to do the best I can to give you at least a superficial orientation to the people and the culture. It's a ridiculous idea. You could live there for years and just begin to understand my country including the 18 proudly distinct major tribes. We all speak Malagasy, of course, but each has its distinct culture and sub-culture, different taboos and dialects, different spirits and folklore. I thought the offer to come here—and the princely compensation—had to be some kind of prank; but one day my checking account was $5,000 richer and an e-ticket appeared on my computer. First class! I've never flown first class before. I could get used to it. I slept half the way from London to Boston on a bed! Woke up and the flight attendant asked me what I wanted for breakfast. What I wanted! So I asked for oatmeal, scrambled eggs and kippers. Guess what. That's exactly what I got—do you believe kippers on a plane? On the way back I'm asking for stewed cumquats and bilberry juice.

"Actually, I don't really understand what you can accomplish, even in a year, on such a huge island. They're also sending a botanist to collect rare orchids and bromeliads along the east coast rainforests. And they hired a third specialist, a local frog expert. Of course you'll all collect a ton of stuff—almost certainly find hundreds of new species. But my island's the size of Texas. It's nearly a thousand miles long. It's really a small continent with dozens of specialized ecosystems. The tallest mountain is over nine thousand feet. And you're going to spend your entire stay in one little corner of the island. Seems like they should have sent 25 people, or maybe even a hundred, and gotten a truly representative sampling of the whole island's plants and animals."

Tryg listened attentively, finishing his lunch and pleased to see a second hefty sandwich disappearing down Mamba's mouth with a second cup of coffee. "good name, Crocodile, Tryg thought, picking up a bent briarwood pipe from the mantle and clamping the stem comfortably between his teeth.

"I think they want just one discovery from me."

13. Tryg as Student

"In the next week, I'm supposed to give you enough information to make you feel comfortable in a completely new culture," Mamba said. "You'll be the only white guy in a tiny village. It's not even a village, really, doesn't even have a name, just some huts and maybe 50 people. You're probably 100 miles or so from a really nice harbor town called Antsiranana on the northern coast. We'll fly there together from Tana.

"The Chapter is antsy as hell to have you working, but spending a few days in Antsiranana is your opportunity to get acclimatized while you're still close to a hospital. Most newcomers get a bad case of diarrhea, or worse.

"Once you move in with the Rock People, you'll be living in the wilds of a tropical rain forest, six miles from Beramanja, the nearest town: it has a single pay phone and a mailbox, but no gas station, no restaurant, no permanent market, no doctor. But every Saturday, weather permitting, the place comes alive with a kind of farmer's market. You'll wonder where all the people came from.

"Three years ago I spent my year-long sabbatical exploring my home island. I spent five days in your village. St. James practically lit up when I told him. I'll go through the photos of my journey and e-mail you ones of the villagers. I bet they'll get a kick out of seeing them. They might remember me; I was the crazy bug man always on the lookout for weevils.

"For the next year, you'll be sleeping under a mosquito net. When you travel anywhere for an overnight stay, carry a treated mosquito net with you; even some of the best hotels don't always provide netting. The Chapter has thought of about everything. Every three months, change your net for a new one, treated with permethrin. Madagascar has its share of diseases including malaria, cholera, bilharzias and rabies, most often from lemurs. But the most likely danger is infection. You'll be provided with a large first-aid kit. It's got an antibiotic powder and some plaster stuff to keep it in place. Every time you get a scratch, bite or puncture, use the stuff. You'll need it almost every day. Wait till you see the trees and bushes. Seems like half the plants have something nasty in store for you—spines and thorns, irritating sap, soft fuzz that sticks to your skin and itches or burns. One plant shoots little darts at you if you touch it. Having fun yet? Let's go over some of the less pleasant possibilities.

"Nice thing about the capital, where I live—it's 4,000 feet high. They even spray the city for mosquitoes. Even on hot days it cools off at night and it's a lot less humid. You, on the other hand, will be living in the lowlands. You're not going to believe the mosquitoes. Mosquito netting works while you're sleeping, but you'll still get bitten every day. Most of the damn things lie low until late afternoon—then the swarms rise like smoke. I hate 'em. If there's a breeze from the ocean, they're not so bad. But sometimes they're so thick . . . Ugh! You've got a hat with a mosquito net. Don't ever get caught in the afternoon without it. People have suffocated from breathing in a few thousand of the little bastards. Every day, you've got to apply repellent. The Chapter has its own concoction. Smells lovely—like zebu dung sprayed with eucalyptus oil. Mosquitoes seem to favor feet and ankles, so wear long pants and socks and rub repellent over the socks."

"Lovely," Tryg grumbled. Mamba flashed his white teeth and continued regaling his host with stories of leeches and scorpions, crocodiles and sweat flies.

"There are dozens of parasites that can enter your feet, especially if you're wading in ponds. Don't ever go barefoot, even on the ocean beach. When you unpack, look for the rubber booties. Even those may not protect you against coral or urchin spines. There are plenty of nasties on the beaches too. Sea snakes rarely bite swimmers, but their venom can be deadly. There are also rays, jellyfish and fish with poisonous spines. If there's a real emergency, The Chapter will send a helicopter from the nearby island of Nosy Be. The worst danger may be cone shells. I noticed you have a nice little collection in your cabinet."

"They're from the Great Barrier Reef," Tryg said. "Picked 'em up with a spaghetti tong. Some of 'em have a poison spike the size of a guitar pick with two or three barbs. I've read about victims of that neurotoxin. I'll definitely be wearing the rubber booties!"

"What's the old cigar box, Tryg?"

Tryg laughed. "Believe it or not, it's my first insect case! I put bugs in cigar boxes and pinned them with Mom's ordinary straight pins. As you can imagine, most of my boyhood collection finally turned to dust. Finally got my first set of Cornell drawers when I was 14."

Mamba continued describing the diverse flora and fauna, delighting especially in the toxins Tryg was likely to encounter. "Some spiders are considered sacred. Others are protected by tribal taboo. Don't kill a spider without asking your tribal witch doctor. On the other hand, tarantulas are a favorite local food. The natives burn the hairs off, wrap it in a banana leaf and *voila*! You've got a tarantula burrito. Quite a few bugs end up on the dinner plate—lantern flies, caterpillars, grasshoppers, beetle larvae. Once the natives get to know you, they'll invite you to enjoy their delicacies. Hospitality demands you share the fruits of their table so I hope you have an eclectic stomach."

"I can hardly wait," Tryg responded, oozing sarcasm, but also secretly relishing his opportunity. Despite trips to Europe and Australia, he had lived a relatively cloistered, professorial life. Mamba's litany of tropical dangers barely mitigated his enthusiasm.

"I guess by now you've heard some of the stories about your hosts, the Antankarana, the Rock People. Unfortunately, I can't tell you a whole lot about them. The other tribes hold them in very high respect, as if they are somehow particularly spiritual or mysterious. They are more isolated, more secretive. Let me give you just one example. All 18 tribes carve special talismans. Some are supposed to ward off evils like cyclones or swarms of locusts. Some honor ancestors. Tourists love to buy these little carvings, usually of wood or shell or even of stone. It's a cottage industry for most of the tribes. We Malagasy don't worry about selling these carvings because a talisman has no power unless it's given to someone by a friend. Most are used for good: for a harvest or for newlyweds to have children. But the Antankarana refuse to sell their carvings. To them, each one is sacred. The most sought-after talismans are the *ody fiti*, which assure the wearer will find true love. My father gave me an *ody fiti* when I turned 20, and two weeks later I met a cute young thing named Gidro Rasoloson. Two months later we were married. Her French/English name is Claire. Befriend your villagers and the *mpitarika*, the tribal leader, may give you a talisman, hopefully an *ody fiti*. No offense, but you should be married. The Malagasy think an unmarried adult is abnormal. Your unmarried status is far stranger than your white skin. To us, the greatest calling in life is to leave descendants. Hey, maybe you'll find a nice Malagasy girl and settle down, make some babies," Mamba laughed.

"Thanks for the warning," Tryg said. "If I get an *ody fiti*, I'll wait to wear it until I get back to Cambridge. Anything else?"

"All the Malagasy tribes honor ancestors. We don't worship them exactly, but they speak wisdom to us, especially to the tribal elders and the witch doctor or magician. We believe in the immediate presence of dead ancestors (*razana*). In many ways, our tribes are united. More or less, we speak a common language. Except for the few of us who are Christians, we believe in one god—*Andriamanitra*—which is also the word for the silk of funeral shrouds. Study the tombs—we call them *fanesy*. The sacred ground of all tombs is scattered the horns of zebus, sacrificed at funerals. You'll always find our totems and the doors of our homes facing east.

"You must give the greatest respect to the village *hazo manga*—the good tree, usually a giant baobab. The oldest baobabs are maybe 400 years old—no way to tell for sure because a baobab doesn't have growth rings. The sacred village tree is protected by the *mpisoro*, the oldest family member in the village. Each tribe has its own particular customs—watch what they do. The night of every full moon, my tribe spreads zebu blood on the bark of our *hazo manga*.

"The Rock People are regarded as the most mystical and mysterious of all the tribes. They've discovered hundreds of *fanfody*, herbal remedies. They don't suffer from malaria or parasites that afflict so many of our people. Their knowledge of herbal medicine is passed on from one honored wise man to another. For years visiting scientists and even members of other tribes have tried to cajole them to reveal their secrets, but it is *fady*—taboo—for them to share their magic, their sacred lore, outside the Antankarana tribe. Every few generations there's a very special *ombiasy*; he is blessed with a magical gift. Supposedly he stays young and lives as long as the *hazo mango*, the sacred baobab tree of the village."

"I've heard those stories, too. The Chapter gave me some documents when I was in London. I think St James may actually believe the legends. Or at least, he's not going to miss a chance for me to discover this secret fountain of youth."

"Ridiculous," laughed Mamba. "No scientist could seriously believe these myths. Wait a minute." Mamba continued his deep contagious chuckling.

"But suppose, just suppose there's some truth to these stories?" What then? What would our world be like if the world's richest people could stay young and healthy for an extra hundred years?"

14. Final Days in Cambridge

The next days passed far too quickly for Tryg. He was an attentive student, but had much to learn. He took notes and saved them on his laptop. He learned some basics of the Malagasy language paying particular attention to native traditions, especially the taboos. Despite Mamba's warnings about parasites and scorpions, Tryg could hardly wait to live in a tropical rainforest among such incredible diversity of unique species. On one island there were an estimated 200,000 species, three-fourths of them insects. He knew the estimates fell far short of reality. Every tropical site ever studied had yielded astounding new discoveries. He was ready for the collecting. But what about the people, the culture, the myriad challenges of everyday life? Each day he felt more eager and more overwhelmed.

Mamba assured him that with 100 Malagasy words he'd be able to communicate his basic needs with the Rock People. Tryg started learning an essential vocabulary and practicing the words with his mentor:

Misaotra	thank you
Veloma	goodbye
Manao ahoana	hello
Tsara	good
Aza fady	please
Fontsy	banana
Omby	cattle
Akoho	chicken
Iza no anasanao?	What's your name?

Mba laupio aho!	Please help me
Atody	eggs
Mandehana	Go away!

"Uncle!" Tryg cried, laughing after a particularly vigorous session. "Let's take a break." He picked up his pipe and drew in a contented breath from the unlit tobacco. "You know what I really want to know, Mamba, me friend?"

"What's that?"

"What are the people really like? I mean, I know they're poor, certainly terribly poor by Western standards. But if I'm going to be living with them for a year, I'd like to, you know, fit in. That's stupid isn't it? I'll never fit in. I'll be another rich white guy living in a cabin. I've got electricity, a refrigerator and stove and a flush toilet, and a computer for God's sake. While they're planting rice and herding their cattle and growing yaro, I'll be wrapping up bugs. Do you think there's any way I could actually get to be friends with the Rock People?"

"To be honest, Tryg, I don't know. For centuries the Malagasy tribes have managed to hold our fragile culture together. White men have raped our women, taken over our ports, cut down our forests. They own all the best beaches and restaurants, the shops and produce. They control the banks, the mines, the tourism. In the last few decades, white men have shipped out millions of board feet of our exotic lumber and tons of minerals and vanilla beans, especially to France. Meanwhile, the Malagasy people have actually grown poorer. Fresh water streams are now filled with red silt or may be dry gulches. Most of the fresh water fish are gone. Traditional native lands keep shrinking as trees fall and developers construct luxury apartments along prime beachfront. Let's face it, the *fotsy lehilahy*—white man—has destroyed much of our country. Even the national parks are protected, not so much for us, but for the tourists who come to see lemurs."

"Well that's just great," Tryg grumbled. "There must be something I can do to build a bond of friendship. I'm not just a tourist. I'm going to be there for a year."

"O.K., now let me tell you the good news. The Malagasy are about the friendliest people in the world. For some reason we're still prone to be naïve and trusting. Give us a little time to really know you, and you become our friend. But how true that is for the more secretive Rock People I don't know. I know you'll be kind and generous. You want to be part of their lives. And you're lucky. A few of the tribe speak some English and most know French. Despite their relative insularity, your little village is not as isolated as you might think. After all, they live on the ocean only 30 miles across the water from Nosy Be, a resort island for the world's rich and beautiful. A French Catholic missionary lived in your village for half a dozen years."

Armagnac served, fire refreshed with another log, Mamba continued. "No offense, my friend, but I know you lost your wife a couple of years ago. You're still grieving. I completely understand. But don't expect the Malagassies to relate to your grief. We mourn for a day or two, bury our dead, prepare a banquet and then get on with our lives. If you were a Malagasy, your wife wouldn't really be dead. She'd now be part of your ancestors. She'd speak to you, give you advice and even protect you. She'd join a family of ancestors going back to our earliest history. When you die, she will be there, waiting for you, and you will join your entire tribe of ancestors, linked to your ancient family, to your living tribe and even to those yet unborn.

"That's just one way the Malagasy are different from the West. We live in terrible poverty and die of a dozen preventable diseases. But look at our faces. We're a profoundly joyful people; as you'll see, we're almost always smiling. We sing and dance and tell stories every night. We work damn hard, but sing as we plant rice or harvest manioc.

"You're white. We're black. Everywhere you go people will call out, *vazaha!* 'white foreigner.' But it's not your color that makes you an outsider. It's two hundred years of colonial conquest. It's not you personally; it's your ancestors. You want to be their friend. But why are you really there? You're going to collect a bunch of bugs and then you're going away. But my guess is they'll quickly invite you into their lives. You're not like a tourist trying to buy some fruit or a carving or a gem. You'll be living with them. The first time they invite you for a meal, you'll know you're on the right track. Breaking bread (well, eating rice) means something very special to them. So does sitting around the fire and listening to their stories. If they invite you to dance, dance. If they offer you their homemade rum, drink the awful stuff. Of course you'll look ridiculous to them. They'll laugh at you, but they'll love your awkwardness. And you'll be another step closer to them."

15. Arrival

Malagasy charm is founded on natural good manners and spontaneous amiability, yet behind this one senses a reserve that makes one feel honoured to be accepted by a Malagasy as a friend.
  - Dervla Murphy, *Muddling Through in Madagascar*

Tryg felt the pressure in his ears and awoke wondering where he was. He sat up and looked out the small oval window at a landscape of red tile roofs. "We're circling Tana," the man next to him announced with obvious pride.

Tryg's mind and body were numb with travel. He hoped Mamba would whisk him to his home and point him straight to a bed. At least it was late afternoon, so with a little luck he'd wake up in the morning and start getting used to a new time zone. As the nimble jet plummeted to the airstrip, Tryg noted four highways converging on the city. The jet taxied for a few minutes to a small, modern terminal.

"Enjoy your stay in Tana," the flight attendant murmured mechanically as Tryg approached the doorway. He was surprised to see a flight of metal stairs leading to the tarmac. A wave of hot air perfumed with overripe flowers competed with the pungent odor of jet fuel making him feel nauseous. If only I hadn't accepted that second drink of orange juice, he thought. He shouldered his carry-on bag and clanked his way down the steps with the other passengers, already feeling uncomfortable in the cloying humidity. "And I'm at four thousand feet," he thought. As he followed others toward the terminal, Mamba greeted him. Though he had been waiting in the full sun, he showed no sign of discomfort.

"Welcome to *Madagasikara*, my friend, Mamba exclaimed, embracing Tryg in an enthusiastic bear hug. "Follow me."

Mamba reached into his shirt pocket and pulled out an ID card. Two uniformed guards with automatic weapons looked at the badge and nodded. "After me, Professor," Mamba said grinning, leaving the line of other passengers. Before Tryg thought to ask where they were going, Mamba approached a set of concrete steps and they walked up alone.

"Shortcut," Mamba said. Tryg followed. At the top of the stairs, Mamba punched four buttons and the metal door creaked open. Cool air! Tryg, already damp with sweat, sighed with relief. Inside was a small room with another uniformed guard sitting at an oak classroom desk.

"Passport, please," the guard said. Two minutes and a stamped passport later, Tryg and his escort entered the main airport and began walking down a short concourse.

"We just bypassed customs," Mamba explained. "All taken care of thanks to The Chapter. Some people spend days getting their visas and work permits. Oh yeah, that reminds me. Here are all your required papers. I don't think anyone will ask for them, but they're already stamped and signed. And here's a million Madagascar dollars." He handed Tryg a stack of bills an inch high, each printed "25,000 Ariaries."

"Before you start shopping for a yacht, it's about $500 U.S. dollars, in case you don't remember the exchange rate," Mamba explained. "Ah, here we are," he said, stopping at gate 5 and handing an envelope to the attendant.

She smiled and said in perfect English, "Your flight will be ready to board in about two hours, Mr. Lindstrom, Mr. Oten."

Tryg groaned. Forget the bed. He had another flight. "But my baggage . . . ," Tryg stammered.

"Oh ye of little faith," Mamba replied. "Have no fear, Mamba is here. Our luggage has already passed through customs and will be transferred to our flight. By the way, the plane to Antsiranana is a bit unpredictable. If they don't sell enough tickets, they simply cancel the flight until the next day. The Chapter has purchased every empty seat to guarantee our trip.

The two sat down on Spartan plastic chairs, Oten talking cheerfully about his beloved city, his pregnant wife and the latest exploits of Mamba Jr. Tryg suddenly felt self-conscious about the large bundle of Malagasy bills. He split the bundle, stuffing half of the currency into his large cargo pants pocket and the rest into his small carry-on bag. "I never put all my eggs in one basket," he explained.

Mamba continued talking about his family, a monologue that soon fell on deaf ears. Tryg was fast asleep.

He had started his year in Madagascar.

16. Antsiranana

Antsiranana means 'where there is salt' but the town is universally known as Diego Suarez after the sailor (described by contemporaries as 'a thief and a murderer who transported Malagasy slaves to India') who secured a tentative foothold here for the king of Portugal in 1543.
- Mark Eveleigh, *Maverick in Madagascar*

Mamba shook his friend gently. "Time to board, Tryg," he said.

Tryg yawned and stretched, disoriented again, bone tired and still a bit queasy. He embraced his friend and promised to send him lots of specimens, especially weevils.

"Wake up and stop the good-byes," Mamba said laughing. "I'm coming with you, remember?"

Tryg smiled sheepishly, trying to shrug off his numbing fatigue, chagrined at having slept during their time together. He stood unsteadily and joined Mamba down a flight of steps to the tarmac which radiated heat waves. The disreputable-looking DC-3 failed to inspire confidence—at least half a century old with small streaks of rust decorating the wings and fuselage at every rivet point. He took a window seat noting that the 12-seater held only four other passengers. Mamba chose a window seat on the opposite side of the aisle. Before the decrepit aircraft rumbled down the airstrip, Tryg had again fallen asleep.

Two hours later Tryg awoke to a sharp pain in his sinus. "Vacuum headache," he muttered," holding his nose and blowing hard as they landed at Antsiranana. Tryg breathed a sigh of relief that the bucket of bolts and rust had survived the journey without mishap. Still groggy, he barely remembered the taxi ride to their hotel or the process of checking in. Mamba effortlessly took care of everything, suggesting they meet in a couple hours for dinner. After a quick shower Tryg gratefully welcomed the bed, noting the mosquito netting. Mamba enjoyed dinner alone as Tryg slept through the night.

The next day was something of a blur for Tryg, as he walked along the streets with Mamba, admiring the jacaranda and coral trees, orchids and towering palms. The heavy scent of ylang ylang and orange blossoms competed with the salty ocean breeze. Barefoot children begged for money, bicycles and rickshaws darted among the cars while the drivers yelled and honked, and occasionally a farmer walked beside a zebu. Tryg, intimidated by the massive curved horns of the cattle, gave the gentle beasts a wide berth to the apparent amusement of their caretakers. They visited a market where Mamba encouraged his protégé to risk a few Malagasy words with the vendors, much to their delight. They sampled a rice dish with boiled fish and any fruit they could peel—mango, a small sweet banana and a grapefruit with bright green flesh. Mamba insisted Tryg sample the ubiquitous burned rice tea instead of the tempting cappuccino featured at several French bistros. They wandered until early evening, admiring the yachts and cruise ships at the harbor. Mamba constantly challenged Tryg by speaking Malagasy, pleased to discover his pupil had already mastered many short sentences:

Afaka anampy ahy ve ianao?	Do you speak English?
Iza no anaranao?	What's your name?
Rats ny andro.	The weather is beautiful
Ho avy ny orana.	It's going to rain
Misy poisina ve io?	Is it poisonous?
Enbto dokotera aho.	Take me to a doctor.

Awaking refreshed the next morning Tryg looked out the window of his comfortable room to a spectacular view of Diego Bay. Luxury yachts glistened in the morning sun. He felt refreshed and eager to walk again. Rather than eat breakfast at the hotel, he invited Mamba to join him and take their chances. The concierge proffered several suggestions.

This time Tryg paid closer attention to the city. The French influence was obvious, from large brick colonial buildings to the road signs and patisseries. Despite Mamba's good natured insistence that Tryg try native fare, they stopped at Boulangerie Amicale for a *pain au chocolat* and a double cappuccino. Tryg was surprised at the international flavor of Antsiranana. Strolling along Rue du Suffren, they entered a market with Chinese, Indian, Malagasy and Arab stores. As the only white face in the market, Tryg frequently heard children shouting *vazaha*.

Two full days in Madagascar (*Madagasikara* Tryg reminded himself) and no dysentery. Enough sightseeing, he thought, eager to travel to his village and move into his new home. "I'm ready, me friend," Tryg declared. "Will you take me to my village in the morning?"

"Better get a cappuccino at breakfast, then. It'll be your last one for a few months."

17. "Home, James"

'What are the roads like from point A to point B?' we enquired.

'Mon dieu! Don't even attempt it!' our informant cried, recoiling in horror at the thought. 'Pot holes the size of wine casks and in places the road completely disappears.'
- Gerald Durrell, *The Aye-Aye and I*

The next morning, Tryg awoke early and returned to the bakery for his last cup of cappuccino while Mamba enjoyed the hotel's buffet breakfast with rice and crayfish. By the time Tryg returned, Mamba had secured the rental vehicle, a Willy's Jeep of unknown age and indiscriminate color. Mamba unceremoniously piled Tryg's bags in the back and they were off. Mamba drove skillfully through the crowded street, dodging bicycles, pedestrians, rickshaws and pushcarts. They soon entered Highway 6. Tryg was pleased: the two-lane road was paved and they were cruising at 90 kilometers an hour. But shortly the "cruise" slowed to a crawl for a zebu hauling a wooden cart filled with bags of rice. Then the pavement disappeared without warning for half a mile as they bounced over teeth-jarring moguls of eroded soil, though there was no sign of road construction vehicles; back to pavement as they came to a small town where they were forced to drive onto the curb to let an overloaded logging truck pass. Then back to the open road. The trip was a maddening series of interruptions and detours. The Jeep with canvas top and doors and faded plastic windows rattled noisily in the wind, the windshield providing the only clear view. Tryg wanted to ask a hundred questions, but the wind and road noise made conversation impossible; so he made himself as comfortable as possible and took in the scenery.

To his right Tryg kept glimpsing signs for Montagne d'Ambre National Park and decided to spend a couple of days there as soon as he was able to take a vacation. Every few miles he saw road signs to enticing sights like Sacre Lac and Ankara Caves.

As he sat back and observed, Tryg began to feel depressed. Mile after mile of barren red soil, bleached tree trunks and a road scarred with deeply eroded gullies carried a steady stream of logging trucks headed north with exotic woods. Every stream they crossed was red with eroding silt. Tryg doubted if fish or frogs could survive in the silty water; the people now had to rely entirely on wells or rainwater.

It was nearly noon when they arrived at Ambilobe. They stopped for welcome bottles of chilled water and a heaping plate of steaming white rice. Tryg was beginning to struggle with the heat and dust, the incessant jarring and noise, marveling at Mamba who had barely broken a sweat. Still, Tryg was the first to clamber back into the Jeep, hoping the windy drive would mitigate the oppressive heat.

The road, unbelievably, deteriorated even further over the next 20 miles, the Jeep bouncing over bumps and cracks and dodging potholes. Periodically, the pavement simply disappeared and they followed tracks across red soil. Stopping for a few minutes to stretch their legs, they each drank lukewarm water deeply from a large weathered canvas canteen.

"Can I ask you a personal question, Tryg?"

"Of course, anything. But I reserve the right to evade a response." He sat on a small oasis of green in the shade of a baobab.

"How'd you meet Moira? You *vazaha* somehow manage to find love without magic."

Tryg smiled enigmatically. "I was fishing at my very favorite secret place in Montana: Kingfisher Creek. The only way to get there is an intermittent trail and steep hike that takes a couple of strenuous hours. I always considered it my own private domain. I'd set up my tent, gather firewood and then go fishing for dinner, having the meadow to myself. It's one of the most beautiful places on earth—a huge meadow of deep grass surrounded by aspen with the small, clear stream winding through beaver ponds full of brookies.

"Well anyway, I set up my tent, rolled out my sleeping bag and gathered plenty of dry wood. As the sun began to set, I got out my trusty four-piece bamboo fishing pole and headed for the stream. Not sure you'd like fishing the way I do, *ny namanao*. I wear cargo shorts and tennis shoes and wade into the icy-cold Montana streams." Tryg chuckled as Mamba shivered impulsively. "Most people use waders to stay dry and warm. But there's no way I was going to lug heavy waders in my backpack with all my other gear. Got to admit, the first couple of minutes take a little getting used to, but soon I was casting upstream and watching my fly drift along the far bank.

"I started catching fish—10, 12-inchers. I had plenty of time to hook a 'keeper,' so I released them and continued downstream. Just when I got to my favorite deep hole I cast too far and the fly landed on the grass on the other side. I gently pulled the line, hoping not to snag in the grass and scare the fish. The fly cooperated and dropped right into the pool.

"Wham! I caught a dandy. The fish bolted straight downstream, the reel spinning. I moved to shallow water and followed downstream, thrilled by the powerful tug of a big trout. As I came around the bend there was a huge logjam, my favorite kind of fishing spot. Fish seem to congregate in the whirlpool in front of the logs, but mine was heading straight for the logs to snag the line and pull free. It doesn't take much to snap a four-pound leader, and big trout seem to know just what to do.

"Sure enough, the trout headed straight into the deep pool, the tip of my rod jerking. Then I saw her. Someone was sitting on *my* logjam. Fishing on *my* river. She saw me, stood up, and all hell broke loose. First, one of the logs moved. Then both her feet slipped forward and she began falling backwards in slow motion, landing on her backpack and then both she and the backpack splashing into the river. For a second I kept playing the fish, unwilling to risk losing it; but she was up to her neck in icy water, her backpack bobbing and sinking as it moved downstream.

"What could I do? I lay my rod on the ground and waded in, pulling her from the river and then rescuing her backpack which now weighed about 200 pounds. By the time I got back to my rod, the trout was long gone and it was getting dark. My damsel in distress was soaked head to toe and shivering uncontrollably. Nothing to do but get back to my campsite and light the fire. No way she could safely hike all the way back to her car after dark. Her spare clothes, sleeping bag and backpacking tent were completely soaked; so I told her to go to the far side of the tent, take off all her clothes and then to get in the tent and put on whatever she could find in my backpack. Meanwhile I'd start the campfire. By the time she joined me, the fire was starting to take hold. She was wearing my field jacket and athletic socks with my ground blanket wrapped around her waist, still shaking with cold and looking miserable. It probably didn't help that I broke out laughing.

"She apologized profusely for losing my fish and sat close to the fire warming up while I changed into jeans, already missing my warm jacket. I made a makeshift clothesline from my fly line and hung her jeans, panties, bra, blouse, socks and tennis shoes along with my cargo shorts and underwear. I hung her sleeping bag and the rest of her wet stuff on tree branches. Quite the domestic little scene. We both sat down by the fire and shared a cup of hot chocolate.

'Hungry? I've got three eggs, a potato and two slices of bacon,' I said.

'Starved,' she replied. 'Sounds like you brought that stuff for breakfast. Let's have some fresh trout.'

'Afraid I don't have any,' I said stupidly, careful to keep any hint of blame from my voice.

"She got up and unstrapped the wicker creel from her backpack. 'Will these do?'

"She had three nice rainbows, probably all caught from my personal logjam. While she warmed up I cleaned the fish. Using a strip of bacon to grease the pan and add a little flavor, a bit of salt and pepper and we were set. I sliced half the potato into the pan and we had a royal feast of potatoes, trout and the rest of the hot chocolate."

'Hope you don't mind sharing my tent,' I said. 'Yours is soaked and so is your sleeping bag. We can unzip my sleeping bag and use it for a blanket.'

"For the first time I took a good look at Moira. Her face glowed in the light of the fire—and what a beautiful face it was. She wasn't exactly at her best, dressed in my oversized field jacket, wrapped in a blanket that didn't exactly flatter her figure and her hair sprouting like a random haystack. She wasn't exactly thrilled to be sharing my tent either, but I guess my culinary skills won her over. We talked late into the night and made a makeshift bed. Even the hottest summer days turn into chilly nights on the Kingfisher; and without socks, my feet kept getting cold. So I kept the fire going with fresh wood every couple of hours. That morning Moira scrambled eggs, the last piece of bacon and the rest of the potato. Her jeans were still damp but they warmed in the sun and she put them on for our hike back down the mountain. Five months later we were married. Maybe rainbow trout is my *ody fiti*."

After another jarring hour in the Jeep, Mamba finally pulled off the road at a few decrepit buildings with rusty corrugated roofs. "Beramanja," he announced grinning. In lieu of a road sign, Tryg would have to take his word for it. An air of desertion was marked by a pay phone on a rusted pole, completely exposed to the weather. Tryg didn't know which deserted building served as a weekend post office. They drove slowly, looking for the road to the village of the Rock People. Suddenly Mamba turned onto a narrow red dirt road nearly hidden by dry grass. "I'm pretty sure this is it, Mamba declared." Tryg hoped he was right.

As they headed west, Tryg noticed they were following a small river. That was encouraging. His map showed an unnamed stream passing through Beramanja and entering the Indian Ocean about six miles further where the village should be. Dismayingly, the "road" soon turned into what could generously be described as two roughly parallel trails transversed by ridges, gullies, deep holes and the occasional boulder.

"Are we having fun yet?" Mamba shouted cheerfully after a particularly jarring bounce. The Jeep bottomed out and Tryg began to fear for the oil pan. A cloud of red dust now enveloped them; Tryg pulled his T-shirt over his nose and mouth to breathe in as little of the red dust as possible. He began to dread an asthma attack; his eyes stung, and they were forced to stop every few minutes for the air to clear enough to see. Without benefit of a breeze, the heat and humidity were oppressive. Things got worse when they stopped to move a downed palm tree. Still attached to the roots and too heavy for them to move, Mamba freed it with a machete. Then they tied one end of the massive palm to the bumper hitch and managed edge it over enough to get by.

On they went, creeping over the bumps or scraping bottom as the tires sank into well-worn tracks. Tryg expected to high-center any moment and anticipated hiking the remaining miles. But somehow the intrepid Jeep and its cheerful driver made progress. "We are so lucky," Mamba said, both sympathetic and amused at his colleague's discomfort. "Many days it's raining in the afternoon. We'd probably have to stop until the storm passed over and then try to get through the mud or wait until morning.

Before Tryg had a chance to ponder his "luck," the so-called road plunged steeply downward. Compound low gears and four-wheel drive kept the Jeep moving slowly, but Tryg realized how impossible this trip would be in a rainstorm. They'd probably slide and if the Jeep turned sideways, they'd certainly start rolling. Still, rolling over seemed almost preferable to the choking dust. When they safely reached the bottom of the hill, Tryg turned around to see his luggage buried under a blanket of red.

He brushed dust off the face of his watch and looked at the time: ten after three. They had been driving for more than five hours. Then he heard it. The surf! He could definitely hear the ocean. If his nose hadn't been so filled with dust, he would have smelled it.

"You did it, Crocodile, me boy!" Tryg said, slapping his friend on the back and raising yet another cloud of dust. Then the road simply stopped at a grassy clearing. About 100 yards ahead they could see smoke from several small fires and a few dozen huts on stilts, every door facing east. And here came the villagers running toward them, shouting, *vazaha! vazaha!*

Tryg had arrived.

18. Welcome to the Village

"How about that, Tryg, the official village welcome." Mamba said, even his teeth now stained red. He pointed, "That's gotta be your house."

Tryg saw it too, a brand new prefabricated white box, 20 feet by 40 feet, looking like a mobile home on three-foot stilts. It even had a screened front porch.

As the Jeep pulled up to the front door, Tryg and Mamba were surrounded by a crowd of men, women and shouting children. "Not offense, Tryg, but I've got a long drive back to Antsiranana. I'll be flying back to Tana in the morning. I'd like to be back to the hotel before dark. And Doc?"

"What is it my intrepid chauffeur?"

"You're covered in dust," he laughed.

Tryg laughed too. Mamba looked like a dark version of Pigpen, red from head to toe. Tryg unloaded his suitcases and canvas bag as Mamba carefully turned the Jeep around through the eager crowd of villagers. He watched the receding Jeep disappear around a bend and clatter into the distance with a series of anemic but cheerful squawks of the horn. The welcoming committee suddenly grew silent and a pathway opened. An old man emerged from the crowd and held out his hand, uttering a fusillade of Malagasy. Tryg was mortified; he couldn't understand a single word. The old man's grin revealed several missing front teeth. His eyes twinkled as he waited for a response. Wait a minute. *tompoko.* He thought he knew that one, hoping it was some kind of welcome. This must be the village elder. Tryg bowed slightly and held out his hand, saying, "*Manahoana tompoko*." The crowd broke out cheering! Tryg had at least broken the ice.

Unexpectedly, the welcoming committee simply and quietly dispersed, even the elder returning to his hut. Tryg was left standing alone beside his luggage. Maybe they were just giving him a chance to get settled. He brushed himself off until he realized the futility of the effort, picked up his things and walked up the steps to his new home. The space was clean but utterly devoid of personality, his "desk," a plain flat hollow-core door, perhaps seven feet long, supported by wooden bookcases. At the sight of those empty bookcases, Tryg felt a pang of longing for his home library. At least the space gave Tryg a large surface to spread out insects. He took a cursory inventory: small bedroom—mosquito netting in place over the twin bed—closet, kitchen with a small refrigerator, stove and sink. He had electricity, running water, a small clothes washer and a bathroom, Tryg was inordinately relieved to see, equipped as promised with toilet and shower. Four wooden chairs and a small table, four sets of glasses, mugs, dishes and flatware, a small supply of knives, serving spoons, and a stocked pantry—Tryg had to admit, The Chapter was pretty efficient. Opening doors and drawers, he discovered his precious dissecting microscope and camera equipment, portable generator and large batteries, bedding and towels, and several unopened boxes of equipment. On the desktop lay an aluminum case with a cord running to a wall outlet. Tryg opened it to reveal the laptop computer Paulette had described. As he turned on the screen he noticed a faint humming at the back of the house. "Generator," he thought.

Tryg busied himself with unpacking and starting to organize his desk as the sky gradually turned orange, then dark. Suddenly, a little girl rushed into the cabin and grabbed Tryg's hand. Other children tumbled in with excited shouting: "Dokotori, dokotori , come quick! Moon in water. Catching many fish!"

The words made no sense to him, but the tangle of endearing faces storming into his home told him something exciting was going on. He allowed tiny hands to take hold of his, realizing that the girl had just spoken to him in English; the jumbled assembly raced toward the ocean. As he approached the edge of the sea ledge he saw a circle of blue-green light, perhaps 50 feet in diameter, illumining the lagoon, The beach was a flurry of activity as the men dragged their canoes and sailboats into the surf. Tryg had seen bioluminescence before, but this was phenomenal. The glow sent shining spume dancing brightly on the waves.

The underwater glow was a nearly perfect sphere. Even from the cliff he could see slender shadows darting across the light. It seemed as if the entire village was running along the beach, launching a flotilla. With the children` he scrambled down the hillside and joined the excitement. Men, women and children carried spears, bows and arrows, and nets as boat after boat entered the surf. Soon a bounty of wriggling fish began to fill every boat.

Tryg wasn't sure why; but suddenly, in this most foreign of places, he felt profoundly at home.

19. Beginnings

Tryg didn't finish unpacking until the next evening, noting that a fine film of red dust had infiltrated even his suitcases. He had spent the day exploring the village and the beach, watching the barefoot children at play and the women making tea and rice on charcoal fires. He laughed as he undressed; noting the dark red stains on his T-shirt around the neck and armpits. Taking a long refreshing shower, red rivulets swirled around the drain reminding him of the iconic scene in *Psycho*. His closet was already filled with practical work clothes—six sets of tan safari clothes provided by The Chapter. While on the long plane trip from Boston, he had re-read the many pages of instructions. He knew his clothes and even his sheets were impregnated with insect repellent, effective only until washed for the first time. He was admonished to use liquid repellent every day and to consume a regimen of tablets to supplement his numerous inoculations. The treated and filtered tap water in his kitchen sink was safe to drink. All other water needed to be boiled or treated with iodine tablets. Lathered with the disagreeable repellent and dressed in his fresh khakis, he ventured forth to watch the sun disappear into the ocean horizon from the perfect vantage point. It was nearly 100 yards by his count from his bungalow to the edge of a 20-foot cliff, where a steep path led to the beach—tricky but manageable. Large jagged rocks lay below him; the surf pounded the rocks, sending a spray of fine rainbowed mist up the face of the cliff.

Tryg, never comfortable with heights, sat gingerly on the edge, feet dangling, and watched the sun slipping into the sea.

Suddenly the village elder and several others joined Tryg on the cliff edge. He scrambled awkwardly to his feet, delighted to have company. The elder urged, *"tonga, tonga"* gesturing for Tryg to come with him. Tryg recognized the word but just couldn't remember what it meant; he felt a bit like Timmy, urged on by Lassie's insistent barking. Tryg eagerly joined the excited group, amused at their outpouring of enthusiasm. As they hurried toward the village's collection of huts, Tryg couldn't help but notice: everyone looked joyful. The children, all barefoot, ran excitedly, laughing at the white stranger in their midst. Even the elder had a wide smile on his face. The entire village seemed to be gathered around a blazing bonfire. The elder took his seat on a small cushion by the fire, motioning Tryg to join him as the villagers took their places, encircling the fire.

Soon a woman brought the elder and Tryg each a clay cup of burnt rice tea. "Guess it's time for me to get used to it," Tryg thought. He was pleasantly surprised by the sweet flavor, discovering the wonder of fresh vanilla beans. As Tryg sat, each family in turn came up to him, bowed and greeted him in Malagasy. Most often the elder male's greeting was *"manahoana, tompoko,"* to which Tryg responded *"Tsara fa misaotra,"* evoking spontaneous laughter from everyone within hearing. Tryg was mortified. He thought he was saying something like, "fine, thank you" to their "Hello, how are you?" but feared his response might be something idiotic, like "I'm a lemur."

Finally a little boy and a familiar girl approached Tryg shyly. The little girl spoke, "Hello, Dokotori Lindstrom."

"What's your name, sweetheart?" Tryg said in surprise, remembering Mamba had told him some of the villagers knew English and many knew French.

"I'm Raozy. *Mpitarika* says my brother Rano and me are suppose to help you because we learn Engliss."

"Thank you, Raozy, and please thank *mpitarika* for me. My Malagasy is terrible. Is that why people laugh when I say *Tsara fa misaotra?*"

"Oh no, mister *dokotori*," she giggled. "We laugh because we so happy you speak to us in Malagasy."

Raozy and Rano moved aside, making way for the others until Tryg had apparently met everyone. When the elder stood up, the whole village rose to its feet. *Mpitarika* said *"Tonga soa, vazaha. Tafandria mandry* (Welcome, white stranger, have a good night)." Without further ceremony the villagers dispersed.

Tryg found it particularly gratifying to be welcomed by a tribe acknowledged as secretive, even mysterious. From the very first day the Rock People had accepted him with apparently genuine friendliness. He had no intention of betraying their friendship by probing their secrets, especially about any magical beetle. Whatever they cared to share with him, he'd be content to listen.

20. Garrote

Three men huddled around the campfire's dancing flames and kaleidoscopic coals on a sultry, moonlit night. A distant jaguar screamed. Frog colonies chirruped, grunted, quacked and giggled from the nearby stream. The fish rat's scaly eight-inch tail twitched as it disappeared inside the anaconda's unhinged jaw. Cloying, humid air reeked of mildew, overripe flowers and fresh asparagus. Despite the relief provided by the fire's acrid smoke, mosquitoes, gnats and biting flies pestered them. The two white men were dressed in identical jungle fatigues, one wearing a green beret, his companion, an Australian bush hat. Under the headgear, similarities ended abruptly. Marvin Winter's chiseled features, deeply tanned face, robust physique and cold eyes suggested years of combat duty. While on a mission, he insisted on the title, "Sergeant." His partner, Colgate, his bush hat limp with sweat, looked uncomfortable and out of place, the impression accentuated by an incongruous cadmium-white coating of zinc oxide on his sunburned nose. Angry welts on his forehead and narrow cheeks competed with a peeling sunburn for the deepest shades of pink. If only he hadn't ignored his supply of sun block and The Chapter's own brand of vile-smelling insect repellent.

The third man was barely five feet tall and naked except for a palm-frond penis sheath. His teeth were as brown as his skin; geometric dark blue tattoos on left cheek and nose identified him as the tribal shaman, the opposite cheek pierced by half a dozen quills. Like other adults in his village, his stunted fingers and deformed hands showed the ravages of Amazonian chiggers. A curved wild boar tusk emerged from each nostril.

Sergeant sat in silence, slowly chewing a piece of roast peccary and staring rudely with open distaste at the witch doctor's nose and facsimile erection. He wondered without genuine curiosity if there were porcupines in the jungle. He was almost equally repelled by his scrawny wimp of a partner. "God damn ethno-freaking-biologist," he spat under his breath. He couldn't understand a word of the primitive gibberish and grunts masquerading for a language, and wished he were back in the village where he could at least gawk at the naked women with relative impunity through mirrored sunglasses. Some of the younger ones were actually damn good looking. Why did they have to scar their faces before they got married? He gingerly tore another piece of simmering meat suspended above the coals. He would have liked some salt or better yet, his favorite brand of fiery barbecue sauce. But he had ingested worse jungle fare—far worse. Thank god they didn't have to eat boiled monkey again, ugh! These creepy spooks had burned off the fur and then boiled the animal whole including the guts and head.

Colgate sat close to the small man, listening attentively and encouraging their tribal host to tell yet another story. He and the shaman had been talking for two interminable days and nights.

Yesterday the visitors had presented the tribe with six live chickens, 10 pounds of beef jerky and a dozen ceramic arrow points. To the Mayoruna these were princely gifts. Sergeant had hoped he'd at least get laid as a reward. But every man in the village carried a bow and arrows or a spear and made it clear their women were off limits. Besides, that faggot St. James had given Sergeant very precise instructions. Find some damned sacred healing flower, bring back a sample, destroy the rest and return to Miami as quickly as possible. Sergeant's reputation had invoked St. James's stern, condescending warning: "Screw around on your own time." Sergeant had entertained pleasant thoughts of ramming his employer's head into his oversized executive desk. He imagined the sound of bone crunching on the shiny wood, front teeth marring the too-perfect patina, followed by the splatter of blood and the terrified scream of the pretty boy. Sergeant still seethed with hatred.

This was Sergeant's fifth mission with his panty-waisted translator. Why didn't they send another military man, someone handy with an

M-16? Still, the previous missions had been cakewalks, earning him nice bonuses. Last month ago, the duo had presented another jungle village with a few gifts and their witch doctor had obligingly led them to a patch of gooey purple slime growing at the base of a tree. Simple as that! They got their sample of the rare fungus, sprayed the rest with bleach and safely boarded a helicopter half an hour later. But this shaman apparently needed more coaxing. "Probably holding out for more gifts, the greedy little bugger."

This afternoon they had left the village hoping for better results from a private meeting, a friendly little barbecue and campout. Now, with each passing hour, Sergeant grew angrier. He stuffed a large pinch of Copenhagen into his cheek and spat into the coals, enjoying Colgate's effete grimace, daring him to say anything. Sergeant half expected the other two to break out the marshmallows and start singing *kumbayah*. While the pig simmered, they had begun drinking vodka. All day the witch doctor had told stories as they passed the communal bottle. The white men pretended to drink freely, but sucked a sip of air from the bottle before tipping it to drink, releasing bubbles. The witch doctor *had* to be drunk by now, Sergeant thought—the liter bottle was nearly empty.

Suddenly the shaman jumped to his feet with a look of understanding on his face and led his guests down a dark path to the nearby stream. He knelt on the bank and began patting it excitedly. Sergeant turned on a small flashlight, illuminating a patch of lush green moss embroidered with tiny pointed red flowers. Responding to the shaman's words, the translator spoke the first three English words of the evening: "This is it."

Sergeant pulled a serrated black combat knife from a sheath secured to his jungle boot and carved a six-inch cube of the moss from the bank, slipping it into an orange gas-permeable plastic bag. Their two days of gifts and drinking had finally paid off.

Colgate bowed in respect to the witch doctor, thanking him. Then the three returned to the fading campfire. As the others resumed drinking, Sergeant seemed to disappear into the shadows. Then, in one practiced, fluid motion, he drew a black braided cord from his pocket and wrapped it around the shaman's neck with fierce brutality, driving a knee into the small man's spine with a sickening crunch as he pulled backwards on the cord. The shaman kicked his feet violently, sending a shower of sparks into the air. His tongue protruded, saliva flowing freely and his eyes bulged horribly, an arc of urine leaping into the air in a flash of reflected firelight.

"No! No! What the hell are you doing!" Colgate screamed in disbelief and horror, his protest already too late. The struggle had lasted for only a few seconds as the garrote crushed windpipe, carotid arteries and the jugular. A stream of bubbly pink saliva poured from the shaman's mouth; then Sergeant simply dropped the lifeless body. The soldier preferred his custom-designed weapon to messy commando-issue piano-wire garrotes that could easily decapitate a man. His braided cord seldom drew blood and was easy to retrieve for the next execution. He calmly coiled the cord around the wooden handles and returned it to his pocket.

"Shut up, Colgate," he snarled to his shaking partner. "Or maybe you'd like to join your little buddy. We got what we were looking for. Who needs the little creep?"

Colgate cowered, his hands shaking. "You better hope no one followed us," Colgate returned, terrified by his partner's threat and looking around with growing anxiety, "or we'll both have poison darts in our necks. That was a stupid-ass thing you did. Why did you have to kill him? You don't have a clue why we're here. The Chapter has spent two years gaining the trust of local tribes. These primitive societies go back 10,000 years. They understand thousands of rainforest plants and hundreds of herbal remedies. *That's* why we're here, god damn it! To bring back their secrets. You've ruined everything, Marvin. We'll be lucky to escape with our lives."

The soldier grumbled, patting the ominous black automatic rifle slung across his massive chest and clenching his right hand into an ominous fist. He welcomed the adrenaline rush and the prospect of emptying a 30-round banana clip into a bunch of savages.

"You're such a cowardly little pussy. There are plenty more tribes of these little black bastards. We better destroy the rest of the moss and get the hell out of here. And one more thing—call me Sergeant."

Both men returned along the pathway to the stream bank and emptied their aluminum canisters of kerosene over the bank of moss. "How do we know this is the only source?" Sergeant asked.

Colgate answered bitterly, "We don't, Sherlock. We'll just have to take the shaman's word for it. I can't believe you killed him. You think you're still fighting in Viet Nam? He's a human being for god's sake. Doesn't that mean anything you? Besides, he might have had so much more to tell us. St. James is going to go ballistic. We'll probably both be fired or worse. This is my last mission with you, Sergeant. And if this moss isn't what we think it is, you're S O L. I'm sure as hell not going to take the blame."

"Shut up, Colgate," he growled, although disarmed at the suggestion that the moss might not be what they had been looking for. "Who would ever come back to this hellhole, anyway? Let's get rid of the body. St. James is never going to know about this," he threatened. Colgate knew he didn't dare to argue; he just wanted to get out of there and away from Sergeant forever. I'll set the igniter for 30 minutes. That'll give us plenty of time to get back to the chopper."

"Wait'll the boys see this," Sergeant thought, patting the outline of the shaman's penis sheath in his field jacket pocket.

21. First E-mail from Paulette

Tryg returned to his pre-fab home feeling warmly welcomed. He was eager to begin exploring—there was so much to see. He could walk along the ocean beach or enter a nearly pristine dense jungle that so far had evaded the intrusion of loggers, and set up his collecting strategies. He walked up the steps and entered the hut. "Guess I'll call it my *cabin*," he thought, switching on the overhead light—too bright! A floor lamp in the corner was better. He got out his essential two-volume *A New Malagasy-English Dictionary* and looked up a few words. *Tonga.* Of course! It meant "come" and "to arrive." He wasn't sure if they had been asking him to come with them or if they were calling him a newcomer. So much to learn. He read a little further: *tonga elatra* was a "newly winged bird." "Well, I guess that's me," he thought. *Tonga feo* was the "first perfect crow of a rooster." Then he thought of the beautiful little kids, Raozy and Rano. "Wonder if I can find their names?" he wondered. Sure enough, he found both names. *Raozy* meant "rose flower." Tryg smiled. The name fit her perfectly. Her brother's name, *Rano,* meant "water." The definition continued: "a child that dies under two years of age; a disease supposed to arise from water." Why would parents give such a name to a child? Then Tryg remembered Mamba's words about how a name could protect someone from his or her namesake.

The computer on his desk was glowing; a click on the Internet icon showed 27 e-mails! He sat at the large desk and began reading. The Chapter welcomed him to his assignment—deleted; The Chapter wanted to know when he had arrived (He responded with a couple of sentences.); his two Chapter colleagues from Harvard (one in New

Guinea; one in Hawaii) sent brief greetings (He returned the same.); Mamba had already sent a welcome letter, happy to be home, his wife due in a couple of weeks. (He responded.); his department office assistant assured him she'd take care of everything for him, especially any parcels of insect specimens; his Harvard replacement, Dr. Adam Pettibone, complained about his "disrespectful students—not at all what he had expected." Tryg tabled his response until he had better control of his indignation. How dare they assign his classes to that insufferable idiot Pettibone!

He was disappointed—nothing from Paulette. "Dummy!" he said aloud, remembering the switcher. He was glad he had packed it in a small zip-lock bag; at least he owned *something* that was dust-free. He took out the thin silver case and clicked it open, taking out the switcher and plugging it into a small slot on the side of the computer. The screen went dark for just a second and then reopened. There it was, the bumblebee icon. He clicked on the bee and another e-mail site appeared with a single message. It was from Paulette. "Who else?" he thought. "She's the only one who can communicate with me in 'top secret' mode."

Tryg opened the e-mail:

Dear Tryg,

I have some bad news. Interpol is investigating a murder in the Amazon basin. A tribal shaman was found in a shallow grave. The tribe identified him by two boar tusks near the skull. The natives say two white men had been at their village asking about their sacred healing plants. We suspect they were agents from The Chapter. However, these tribes often go to war against one another and when they do, they especially try to kill the shaman. We've lost any chance of forensic evidence since the tribe placed the shaman's remains on a funeral pyre. Still, we're more than just suspicious of The Chapter. The same night that the shaman disappeared, the two white men left the village.

Maybe The Chapter has a maverick on its hands. We're watching several suspects closely, including your old school chum Marvin Winter. He was one of The Chapter's two men in Peru when the shaman was killed.

There's no reason to think you or any other scientist is in any danger. You're helping The Chapter to find miracle cures. But if you do find some kind of elixir of youth, let me know right away. I suspect they'd do almost anything to get their hands on it.

You now have a second person you can communicate with on the secure switcher mode: Mamba. I know he has become a friend. He may be a valuable resource to you. He has a copy of this e-mail and a secure switcher on his computer.

Tryg started typing:

Dear spy leader.

I think St. James is a sleaze, but doubt if he'd condone murder. Doesn't make sense he'd risk his fame and fortune. Someone who dresses so impeccably doesn't want a loose cannon out there putting his dreams at risk. He stands to make billions from the drugs and herbs he's testing, why risk everything by becoming some kind of modern-day gangster. More than that, St. James should want to cultivate good relationships with the shamans; they are his best guide to the natural remedies he's seeking. The murder is really disturbing. In case you don't know, Marvin's the one I was talking to when you entered the Ritz Club, trying to convince me to accept The Chapter's offer. He's a bit of a brute. Still, I can't imagine him killing anyone. There's something cowardly about him.

I'm not too concerned about some vague danger from The Chapter. I've got more immediate worries: asthma, crocodiles, and a hundred nasty tropical diseases and parasites. Thank you for adding Mamba to my secure communications list. He's become a good friend. I'm trying to convince him to name his next baby Tryg Mud Dauber Oten.

If St. James really expects me to find the fountain of youth, he's going to be very unhappy with me. The story's a crock. However, if I do discover a secret elixir and turn into a little boy, you'll be the first to know. And I promise you, The Chapter will never get the formula – maybe I should give it to Woody Allen who said something like, "I don't want to achieve immortality through my work, I want to achieve it through not dying."

I'm sure they'll develop a bunch of new medicines from Madagascar. There is just so much to discover. But this island is under extreme stress. In nearly a hundred miles of driving from Antsiranana to my village, I saw what was once a tropical rainforest turned into eroding red soil and tree trunks. It's heart-rending. The island is dying. I can see why The Chapter wants to collect everything it can before the unique flora and fauna here is destroyed forever.

By the way, the Rock People have welcomed me as an old friend. I just arrived and have already enjoyed my first tea party—a cup of rice tea with my villagers Try this: burn a little rice in a saucepan, then add a cup of water, bring to a boil, add a small piece of a fresh vanilla bean and you have Malagasy tea. Maybe add a bit of their ylang ylang honey that tastes like butterscotch. Tea is more than the national drink to the Malagasy; it's a sign of their hospitality. I actually feel as if I'm among friends. If I could just stop craving cappuccino. Guess I better get used to my new home.

Tomorrow I start hunting—bugs, not crocodiles!

P.S., When I get back to Harvard, will you go out to dinner with me? And wear that green gown again?

Your humble minion,
Tryg

Tryg rummaged around a closet until he found fitted sheets and a light blanket. When he returned to shut down the computer, the bumblebee icon was flashing on the screen! Tryg felt unexpectedly pleased—Paulette had already answered him. He felt, well, *connected.*

I'm afraid I have more bad news regarding Crummy and Robertson. Remember how some people died of cancer after taking the arthritis herb? Turns out there were no carcinogens in the beetle. They had a legit cure for arthritis! But some of the capsules we confiscated were laced with powerful carcinogens. No doubt about it; the tampering was deliberate and malicious. Now The Chapter is making millions on the drug. Follow the money.

Those people who died . . . were murdered.

22. Tryg the Witch Doctor

After spending many weeks with the tribe, Tryg was more convinced than ever that the Rock People were typical, impoverished Malagasy people, with a tragically short life expectancy of 55 years. He sent St. James a pointed e-mail confirming that the fountain-of-youth bug was pure folklore.

Tryg had a huge advantage collecting bugs: his "army" of five local children, especially Raozy and Rano, who brought the professor dozens of insects one or two days a week. In the afternoon, the professor often sat on his screened porch, kids seated at his feet, to examine the bounty: six-inch long katydids and leaf-mimic insects; walking sticks twice that long; ants, bees, wasps, cockroaches—but mostly beetles. He paid his army handsomely by local standards—10 U.S. cents for every accepted insect. Each specimen had to be perfect: six legs, both antennae, perfect wings. On an island where the average family annual income was $270, he regularly doled out $3 to $5 a week to the families of each of his well-trained helpers and matched that amount to the village. Once, Raozy brought an unusual find, a giant stick insect with three normal legs on the right side and three tiny legs on the left. Somehow the creature had lost its left legs and they were now in the process of growing back. Raozy expected her catch to be rejected; instead, he paid her $5. The children knew not to bring any but the most beautiful butterflies or the largest silk moths as these were the most generally studied and collected insects. Tryg kept a few of these specimens for his personal collection, since The Chapter had summarily dismissed lepidoptera as a worthwhile source of medicinal value.

His first few weeks in the village, Tryg had spent many enjoyable hours with his army, teaching them to be gentle with a net and collecting jar. The children soon discovered his special love of bees and wasps, collecting a constant bounty of paper wasps, mud daubers, bright green and blue metallic bees, giant bumble bees and solitary hunting wasps. The children taught him, too. They knew where insect-attracting flowers were in bloom and how to treat the welts Tryg suffered from daily insect bites and stings.

After a time, however, children's nearly constant presence became more distracting than helpful, so Tryg put a small flagpole on his roof. Once every week or two, he raised a green cloth flag—the army was hired! They'd gather with their jars inside Tryg's enclosed porch a couple of hours before sunset. "Dokotera Tryg" dispatched the collectible insects. Tryg carefully credited each child's account for the number of accepted bugs. The families then used their accounts at the Beramanja market to supplement their supplies of rice and fresh produce.

One day three children came charging onto Tryg's porch and began pounding on his door. "Mpampianatra! Mpampianatra!" they cried. "Avy haingana!" ("Teacher, teacher, come quick!")

Tryg swung open the door to his young workers, tears streaming down their faces. "What is it, kids?" he asked, kneeling down on the porch. They didn't understand. He struggled to say something. He tried: "Ratsy (bad)?" It was close enough.

They nodded eagerly all shouting at once. "*Rano, maty!—fanenitra! Avy haingana!*" (Rano is dead! Wasp! Come quick!")

At least Tryg made out that much. Little Rano was dead. Stung by a wasp or maybe a swarm of bees. Conflicting thoughts rushed through his head. Could he have put one of these children in danger? "Oh God," he thought, "please, please help me." Tryg almost followed the children who had bolted outside. Suddenly he rummaged through his medical supplies, remembering the first aid kit that included epi syringes. Grabbing the aluminum case he sprinted after the kids. The pathway was slippery with mud as the three hurried through the now familiar jungle trail. Tryg ignored the slapping of branches that clutched at his clothing and scratched his face. Suddenly the little boy came into view, curled at the side of the trail. Dozens of wasps buzzed angrily around their dull green paper nest, but for some reason were content not to dive bomb Tryg and the children. Tryg opened the case, ripped open a package and without thinking, plunged the small needle into the boy's thigh. He turned the boy's limp body and sighed—the boy was still breathing! He scooped up the child in his arms and began walking as fast as he could back toward his cabin. The kids took turns carrying the first aid kit. All the way back, Tryg continued to assure the children that Rano was fine. He wasn't so sure.

When they reached the cabin, Tryg laid the boy on his bed, covering him with a blanket. "What if the epi was too strong for a child!" he thought, a wave of fear and guilt pounding his chest. He wasn't a doctor. He might have just killed the boy. The children sat on the floor looking at the man with absolute trust in their eyes. He had said Rano would be OK. They all knew "OK." And they believed in the Dokotera. Several angry welts covered the boy's cheeks. Tryg wrapped a few ice cubes in a towel and gently ministered to the frail child, not knowing what else to do.

Then Rano simply opened his eyes. His three mates began yelling with joy, turning the cabin into the scene of a tumultuous celebration and a stream of words he could not hope to understand. Tryg joined them, tears streaming down his face. Half an hour later, the four were sitting on the floor of the covered porch drinking rice tea with milk and honey. The children kept calling Tryg "fanafody lehijali."

As closely as Tryg could figure out, the kids had just proclaimed him witch doctor.

23. Asthma

Tryg breathed in the humid, perfumed air and began coughing. He bent over, hands on his knees, lightheaded from the series of racking coughs. His asthma was becoming a nuisance. Despite his most recent regimen of Symbicort and ProAir, his chest had tightened and breathing grew increasingly labored. Tropical air was a soup of mold spores and grasses, rotting fruit and pungent flowers, airborne bacteria and the ever-present village charcoal smoke. There was no way to isolate whatever was triggering his discomfort. To complicate matters, every few days a dozen new plants might burst into bloom, broadcasting clouds of new pollens and fragrances. Evenings were the worst. When he lay down he began to wheeze, forcing him to sit up most of the night. His peak-flow meter readings had been declining, but after three puffs of ProAir, today's best reading of 225 alarmed him. He knew he was getting into serious trouble.

He reached under his desk and brought out the small gym bag, rummaging for the jar of prednisone tablets and popping three of the small orange tablets into his mouth, grimacing at the vile taste, even worse than the iodine-laced water he forced himself to drink in the field. He downed the rest of his cold rice tea, but the offensive taste lingered.

He regretted waiting so long before starting the steroid, but he hated and feared the effects of prednisone. His worst fear was getting an illness or infection while the steroid suppressed his immune system. But the low reading on the peak flow meter left him little choice. Unfortunately, the magic tablets that brought such welcome relief took three or four days to start making a difference. "I'm too young to be a damn invalid," Tryg thought bitterly, reviewing the little pharmacy of medications in the bag. He smiled ruefully, setting up the nebulizer. As the machine hummed, he began inhaling, wondering how the colorless liquid in the nebulizer disappeared into inhaled mist.

In a few moments the liquid was gone. He turned off the machine and pushed the flow meter dial to zero, inhaling deeply and expelling a pitiful burst of air: no change, 225. He needed to contact The Chapter. He began typing:

Whoever reads these e-mails, greetings. My health has suddenly gotten worse. Peak flow readings have been declining. Dropped from 300 yesterday to 225 this morning. Despite Pro-Air and nebulizer, I'm still at 225. Have oxygen ready and have just started a 15 mg/day prednisone treatment as per my medical instructions. Have never been on this high a dose. I want to stay here—wonderful discoveries almost every day—but am on the verge of returning. Please advise.

Regards,
Tryg

Tryg clicked the "Send" button and began packing the nebulizer. As he zipped up the case, the computer beeped—a response already!

Dr. Lindstrom,

Sorry to hear about the asthma. Please stay put. Help is on the way. We have contacted Dr. Armini in Ambilobe, who will leave first thing tomorrow morning. We also have a dedicated air ambulance on alert at Nose Be. If you need immediate help, type C-400 (our 911 code) to this address and a helicopter will arrive within an hour. In the meantime, please stay inside. Use your oxygen tank if your blood oxygen falls below 90%.

Tryg felt he should be relieved and grateful for the immediate response and assurance of help. Instead, he felt vaguely disturbed at the instant feedback. He was being closely monitored. Creepy. He told himself to chill out; he was getting paranoid of Big Brother. Help was on the way. Stay put. One good thing—his responder mentioned blood oxygen level. Tryg emptied the gym bag. Sure enough, the meter was there in its unopened box. He felt a bit sheepish. He had completely forgotten to monitor his blood oxygen level. He placed the clip over his index finger and watched the numbers bounce around until they settled on 88 percent. He slipped on a mask and began breathing pure oxygen.

A moment later the anonymous responder on the computer screen reprimanded Tryg in no uncertain terms to take better care of himself and keep The Chapter apprised of any health issues. "Asthma can be fatal!" warned his e-mail.

"Great long-distance bedside manner," Tryg grumbled. He just wanted to lie down and sleep. The most discouraging thing about his asthma was the constant fatigue. The rest of the day, Tryg stayed home, coughing up phlegm and meditating self-indulgently on his mortality. So far he had avoided any number of tropical diseases and parasites. Wouldn't it be ironic, he thought, if he died of something as mundane as asthma. His blood oxygen readings quickly jumped to the high 90's. He tried to relax and stay close to the nebulizer and oxygen.

The next morning, an impossibly tall black man arrived on an incongruously small yellow Vespa scooter. A dozen excited children were shouting, running alongside the visitor as he stopped in front of Tryg's home. Towering over Tryg, the stranger introduced himself as Dr. Armini. He had driven at night from Ambilobe to Beramanja in his VW beetle and then continued that morning on the dirt road by scooter, unwilling to brave the notorious rutted venue the village in his car. With little ceremony, the giant administered an injection of adrenaline. Almost immediately Tryg felt a surge of relief, breathing deeply and celebrating the miracle of unlabored breath. Armini also prepared a cup of vile-tasting *amor seco* herbal tea. Why couldn't someone create medicine that tasted like bleu cheese or chocolate chip cookies he thought ruefully—tastes like creosote, even worse than the lingering bitterness of prednisone

The doctor left Tryg with a vial of adrenaline, four syringes, a tin of dark green *amor seco* powder and an unlabeled orange plastic bottle of pills. "Take one of these tonight, Tryg," Armani had insisted. "It's a powerful sleeping pill. You can take another after six hours if you need to. You need sleep. For that matter, so do I after spending last night in my bug. I can hardly wait to get home to my bed."

Moments later he ducked under the doorway and managed to arrange himself on the Vespa, surrounded by what appeared to be every man woman and child in the village. He started the scooter in a cloud of blue smoke and began his teeth-jarring return journey.

Tryg slept comfortably the entire night and awoke refreshed. He was breathing much more comfortably and his congestion was diminishing. His oxygen reading was up to 95 percent; the flow meter read 425, and two days later he managed a respectable 475. The prednisone had begun working.

For now he could stay.

24. Hissing cockroach

"Damn prednisone," Tryg grumbled. He had already endured three nearly sleepless nights. Despite the numbing exhaustion, his calf muscles twitched restlessly and he felt his pulse drumming in his ears. The previous evening, he had reluctantly tried the white sleeping tablet with unsatisfactory results, dozing into nightmarish fits, then jolting awake and pacing the cabin with agitated frustration.

Shortly before sunrise, he had finally collapsed again for some precious unconscious minutes as dawn intruded with the familiar crescendo of jungle cacophony. As he tumbled into bed he downed two tiny white sleeping pills. He hated the thought of yet another chemical surging through his body, perhaps ensnaring him in a web of dependency. But he capitulated for some few essential hours of sleep. The pill was slightly bitter and slightly sweet. He wondered for a moment if it was a placebo—looked like the saccharine tablets his aunt had kept on her kitchen table to sweeten her coffee. Why wasn't the bottle labeled, he wondered. He wasn't prepared for the sudden results. He couldn't keep his eyelids open. They fluttered as he fought against claustrophobic dimming light, wispy strands of blue smoke swirling around his head as the walls tilted. His pipe slid from his lips and fell to the floor with a distant click. Then he saw the familiar visitor on the ceiling and smiled. He had grown quite fond of the omnipresent five-inch hissing cockroach—*Gromphadorrina portentosa*. Portentous was a good name for the clown, hissing like a viper, but perfectly harmless. If he had put together the Latin roots correctly, *Gromphadorrina portentosa* meant something like "pompous spear-nosed old sow." Gotta love the entomologist who had named the critter.

Portentosa was now rearing up like a cobra, waving side to side in warning. But the approaching golden scorpion found nothing fearful in the roach's antics. The translucent hunter scrabbled across the ceiling, proffering no pretense to stealth, scissoring its two oversized claws in a macabre mockery of its swaying victim.

"How can such a heavy scorpion walk on a ceiling?" Tryg wondered. "Run! Run!" he suddenly yelled to the hissing clown, as he reached for the canopy zipper, ready to intervene.

Too late.

"Crunch!" A golden claw reached out, severing the now-silent victim. As the scorpion fed, bits of gore and shining flakes of the hapless cockroach fluttered from the ceiling onto the mosquito netting above Tryg's head, reminding him of insulating Zonolite dust in the attic of his childhood home.

The scorpion took its time, munching piece after piece. Suddenly an ominous silent shadow attracted Tryg's attention at the right foot post of his bed. The sleek, furred creature looked like an Art Nouveau cat come to life. Black as a panther and three feet long, the fossa hugged the post like a lover. She glanced down at Tryg sensuously, with deep red eyes and waving extended claws. In the background a voice whispered vaguely familiar words: "Sudden thin and piercing ray of red from under the drooping lid. . . ." Red eyes. Several species of lemur and sifaka had those same red eyes. For that matter, he had found local red-eyed frogs, chameleons, black cicadas and stalk-eyed flies. While Tryg might be a naturalist, he involuntarily abandoned his emotional detachment: red eyes gave him the creeps. He shuddered with revulsion, waiting for the wicked eyes to radiate their fatal crimson light upon him; but the carnivore cringed in stealth toward the feasting scorpion.

Two rays of crimson light beamed from the fossa's cruel eyes, illumining the aureate scorpion that turned to face the fearsome beast. Tryg watched, mesmerized, as the scorpion raised its deadly curved stinger in defense, dripping yellow venom that sparkled in the red light. In a blur, the fossa's catlike claw grabbed the arachnid and plunged the writhing animal into her eager crushing teeth. Bits of scorpion gore sprayed the canopy. The fossa seemed to be laughing, emitting short hissing pants. Exultant, the fossa spoke: "My teeth are swords, my claws spears."

Then they came. Scores of hissing cockroaches streamed under the front door and through a small crack in the window ledge, scurried up the walls and across the ceiling. The fossa slunk away as countless roaches dropped onto the mosquito netting, lapping up drops of scorpion blood, their hissing growing louder and louder.

Tryg screamed, his voice drowned by the deafening hissing. Small cracks appeared in the walls and liquid golden light began oozing through, flowing down the walls and spreading across the wooden floor. Rays of light poured across the bed, bathing Tryg's face. He struggled to turn away from the piercing glare.

Something wasn't right about the hissing. The pitch began to alternate high to low, high to low. It reminded him of the police sirens in London. With a sudden spasmodic jerk, he awoke, panting and bathed in sweat. The rising sun baked the bedroom. Sirens continued. Tryg gradually recognized the offensive clamor dominating the soundscape. He glanced at the digital clock—6:05. Right on time. He called them six-o'clock cicadas. For the past two weeks, at about this time, the countless millions of newly-hatched cicadas began their siren chorus that drowned out every other sound for miles. One or two hours later the din would abruptly give way to the other tiers of jungle commotion.

Tryg glanced at the ceiling. *Portentosa* hadn't budged.

25. Web

The world's tangled and hieroglyphic beauty
                        - Robert Penn Warren

After nearly three months in the tropics, Tryg still languished in the heat. The nearly daily afternoon rainstorms offered temporary relief, followed by insufferable humidity as soon as the sun came out, mitigated somewhat by a cooling ocean breeze. But today's destination required him to climb determinedly into the jungle, away from the coast. The rain had turned the trail to slippery, ubiquitous red mud. As the trail grew steeper, he slid precariously with every step. Sharp rocks protruded from the mud, waiting to slash open a hand or shatter a knee. Abruptly the trail leveled out as the jungle canopy closed in.

Tryg had to stop for a minute to let his eyes adjust to the dark tunnel ahead. Although the sun was almost directly overhead, the dense jungle canopy blocked out all but isolated rays of light. Moss hung in long streams from overhanging branches, and unidentified creatures scuttled disarmingly with his every step. Bizarre twisting roots grabbed at his ankles; vines, leaves, ferns and cobwebs constantly brushed his face. He moved cautiously, his greatest concern a particularly nasty liana with wicked barbed spines. As soon as a spine drew blood, one could count on an invading army of bedeviling, tormenting, infecting flies, leeches and ants.

Everything was wet. When he ducked under a giant fern leaf or pushed aside orchid-laden lianas, he was drenched anew in water. Bamboo groves often formed an impenetrable wall, and Tryg struggled with claustrophobia. With one careless motion he brushed the back of his hand against a thorn bush and three angry scratches began to bleed, stinging fiercely. "Damn," Tryg groaned. Even the most innocent-looking wounds could turn septic. His destination was only half a mile into the jungle, but his progress was slowing and he began panting. He took out his ProAir and inhaled a puff.

Tryg stopped a moment to take in the infinite variety of green. Every tree trunk was covered in moss, lichen, fungi and mushrooms. He aimlessly broke off a piece of bark; a 10-inch centipede reared up and hissed before darting away. Its fangs were nearly an inch long. He reached for the powerful flashlight hanging from his belt and ran the light slowly up a fern tree. Every few inches the beam revealed a spider or a line of ants, a tiger beetle, a chameleon, a walking stick or a jelly-like purple fungus. He shuddered, remembering his first foolish encounter with one of these fungi whose oozing pores had burned the skin off his right index finger and left an angry purple scar.

The jungle bombarded him with competing odors: vanilla, frangipani, oozing sap reeking of creosote, orchids with perfume of overripe lilies or rotting flesh. Nature was everywhere garbed in hyperbole. Tryg felt overwhelmed, recalling Shelley's phrase: "profuse strains of unpremeditated art."

And the noise! The background sound was always the same: buzzing . . . of innumerable mosquitoes, flies and bees. Layered over that, dozens of birds peeped, squawked, chirped, cawed, laughed, meowed and barked. Lemurs stayed out of sight but screamed, hooted and taunted, sometimes urinating and defecating from the treetops. Many of the orchids looked evil, yellow-brown streaked with lavender. Something lurked under every rock: hissing cockroaches, spiders, giant millipedes and centipedes, spiders and leeches.

He continued walking in the near-darkness, glad for the bright beam of his flashlight. With a start he shuddered, spotting a three-inch black leech crawling over the back of his hand and starting to enter his shirt sleeve. Snapping his finger, the cold heavy leech flew off before it had a chance to attach securely. He hadn't even felt it. His pant cuffs were firmly tied at the ankles so he felt fairly confident that his legs would be spared, but leeches tried to drop on any passing animal with warm blood; Tryg knew he had to keep moving.

The pathway was now so dark he had to turn on the headband light. "How could such an abundance of plants survive in this darkness?" he wondered A green snake dropped from a tree and slithered across the trail. There were more than 90 species of snakes on the island. Mamba had stated with aplomb that even the poisonous ones were "practically harmless" to humans. He continued, hoping he wouldn't have to start hacking away with his machete. So far the most annoying barrier seemed to be the small "Velcro vines" whose tendrils grabbed anything in their paths. When he tried to move them aside or step over a tangled mess, the vines sank countless tiny barbs into fabric and skin. He imagined the tendrils encircling his ankles.

Gradually the trail began to clear; he could see patches of blue sky and sunlight. Then he heard it—the buzzing, a new powerful undertone emerging from the incessant background noises. The villagers had told him to listen for it. It reminded him of high-power electrical cables or a distant small engine. As he moved forward, the newly persistent drone increased. Tryg returned the heavy flashlight to his belt. It was now light and growing warmer. Ahead he spied the village's sacred giant baobab fully six feet in diameter, its trunk carved with concentric circles. At the baobab, the path turned sharply to his right. He walked around the curve and froze, hardly believing his eyes. A few feet ahead, a dense 10-foot high web blocked the path, extending in two directions from palm tree to palm tree, for hundreds of feet. The massive web sparkled with raindrops in the sunlight, like a billion tiny diamonds. At night he might have walked straight into it. The buzzing sound was an almost deafening death cry of thousands upon thousands of hapless insects, victims of a colony of giant orb weaver spiders, whose webs are the strongest on earth.

Tryg approached slowly, fascinated and repulsed at the same time. So close he could touch the silken curtain, he watched the web moving in waves, pulsating with the desperate energy of flies, wasps, beetles, grasshoppers, dragonflies and honeybees struggling to escape. The spiders seemed in no special hurry. Their golden bodies big as a man's thumb, projected an octet of powerful spiked legs. They methodically collected the largest insects, ignoring the millions of tiny ones. One large spider had singled out a dangerous two-inch jet-black hunting wasp with bright red wings. As the weaver advanced, the hunting wasp tried to position her abdomen for a fatal thrust. The spider simply moved to the head of her prisoner and sank lethal fangs at the base of the wasp's neck. The wasp buzzed ferociously, whipping her abdomen desperately, her lethal half-inch stinger impotently thrusting the air. Then the buzzing stopped; the fight was over; the orb weaver began to drink. Tryg approached the web cautiously, clear plastic collecting jar in hand. The spider ignored his advances, feeding on her prey. Heart pounding with fear, Tryg held the mouth of the jar near the giant spider, the lid in the opposite hand. Deftly he closed the jar on the spider, leaving the wasp in the web. He quickly backed away as other spiders began to converge.

Tryg had read about *Nephila madagascariensis*, the Golden Orb Weaver. Queen Victoria had been presented a pair of stockings woven from its web. As he surveyed the massive killing net of spider's silk, he spied a small spread-eagled yellow bird, staring sightlessly. The orb weavers had already turned the finch's insides to liquid and left only a feathered skeleton. Tryg had seen community webs before, but had never heard of spiders dividing their labor. Here, smaller spiders were busy extricating desiccated carcasses from the web, while mature sisters repaired the gaps. Foraging ants and bright orange carrion beetles eagerly removed the jungle floor litter.

Horrified, Tryg turned to his right and paced the perimeter. He was stunned to see a giant jumping rat, two feet long, hanging lifeless and partly skeletonized, covered with flies. Tryg watched as several young spiders worked to free the rodent. It finally dropped to the ground where the opportunistic continuous stream of army ants carried away the spiders' trash.

He gave the lid of his collecting jar an extra tight turn and slid it into a loop on his belt. He didn't wait to observe the fate of the desiccated rat.

26. *Nephila St. James*

Dear Mamba,

I'm sending you a spider. I know you said not to bother you with eight-legged critters, but this Nephila madagascariensis *is truly gigantic. The body is fully 5 cm long. I had no idea they got so huge. You have to see the unbelievable communal web. I'm sending several digital pics. Did you know* Nephila *eats birds and even mammals? Hope I've earned some Bit-o-Honey – finished my last one days ago.*

Regards,
Tryg

My dear professor,

5 cm! That's no Nephila madagascariensis! *You've found a new species, me boy. Last year someone found a giant golden orb weaver in central Madagascar. Named it* Nephila komachi. *Your specimen is a good cm larger than komachi. Thanks for your kind offer to visit the web, but your nightmarish pics are as close as I want to get – that web gives me the creeps. Maybe you'll want to name your new* Nephila *after our arachnidan benefactor, St. James. Send me spiders, you get an e-mail. You want Bit-o-Honey? Send weevils!*

Your friend,
Crocodile

P.S. We've got a locust in Madagascar that kills and eats mice!

27. Battle Plan

Memo
Top secret, encrypted
From: Dr. Benjamin St. James
To: Executive Board, The Chapter

1. *Several major projects ahead of schedule. Refer to enclosed CD with information we can share publicly with our subsidiary investors and the press.*
2. *Newly acquired arthritis remedy a spectacular success. We have isolated the active alkaloid and, eliminated the toxic by-products. I'm sure everyone was pleased with this month's financial distribution.*
3. *Re: Prototype 407, an apparently unique insect protein that destroys selected microbes. The heir-apparent treatment for a wide spectrum of pneumonia-causing bacteria. Expect huge financial returns.*
4. *Re: Prototype 1,366 -- still promising to become blockbuster drug. It's a family of molecules that seeks out and destroys cancer cells without harming other tissues.*
5. *Re: Prototype 2,257, an apparently unique bacteria found in a tropical genus of insects, previously thought impossible to culture in a laboratory. Bacteria act as powerful anti-inflammatory agents.*
6. *Re: Fountain of Youth beetle – still our top priority. No progress to date. Scientist imbedded in Madagascar. Planning to send another interrogation team.*

7. *Success continues on longevity studies of yeast. We have extended the life span of yeast cells up to25-fold by removing genes RAS2 and SCH9.*

8. *Breakthrough research continues on the jellyfish* Turitopsis nutricula. *Mature jellyfish spontaneously return to their immature polyp form and then mature again. It appears this rejuvenation process can be repeated in an endless cycle. We have successfully rejuvenated nematodes, fruit flies, frogs and mice.*

9. *Have initiated trials of nanobot infusions in chimpanzees to repair damaged organs.*

10. *Have applied for experimental treatment of terminal patients waiting for vital organ transplants. Have perfected the technology of growing kidney and heart cells from skin cells. We intend to inject these cells into the human bloodstream in order to rejuvenate aged or damaged kidneys and hearts.*

11. *Continuing research on Methuselah gene in* Drosophila melanogaster.

28. The Chapter Laboratory, Miami

Jimmie Benson stood up and stretched. He was stiff, tired and grouchy. He had been pissed off for two weeks, ever since The Chapter had issued a memo forbidding food and drink in its precious laboratory. Every day for nearly three years, Benson had brought a thermos of coffee and a pocketful of pistachios into the lab. Rumor had it that Benson laced his coffee with Jim Beam. He certainly emitted a suspicious odor of alcohol, or was it just the formaldehyde and benzene or any one of a dozen other chemicals the scientists used daily?

Benson walked down the long aisle of black-topped lab tables, past the electronic microscope, hundreds of Petri dishes and a dozen flat-screen computer monitors. His colleagues, all wearing similar white lab coats, paid him scant attention. Each seemed engrossed in an all-consuming task. Benson wandered to the bank of thousand-gallon aquaria filled with clams and coral and strange-looking fish. He glanced sadly at the collection of tortoises in the next enclosure. "Goddamn zoo," he muttered to no one in particular.

He shuddered as he passed a door labeled "Test animals." Two years ago he had toured the animal laboratory filled with caged mice and rats. Suddenly the room had burst into deafening screams as he approached the chimps and rhesus monkeys. He had never returned.

Finally he stopped at a cluttered lab table with an engraved name plate, "Ivan the Terrible Pogarski"

"Dr. Jimmie! How ya'll doin'?" beamed the round, pink-cheeked face.

"C'mon Pogo. Let's get some lunch. I need a break."

"It's barely 11," Ivan chuckled in mild protest. Of course it's meat loaf Tuesday; always good to hit the cafeteria early. With that, the rotund Ivan hopped to his feet and the Mutt and Jeff duo made their way through three security doors and into the cafeteria.

Not surprisingly, Ivan ordered the veal meat loaf with extra gravy. Then he added French fried sweet potatoes, asparagus, A dinner rolls with extra butter and cherry pie ala mode. Benson took the steamed salmon and a salad. "Watching your girlish figure?" Ivan quipped as they took a table in the empty dining hall.

As soon as they sat down Benson grimaced. "I've had it with this nuthouse," he grumbled. "I'm quitting at the end of the month."

"Quitting!" exclaimed Ivan. "You've got a great job and pullin' down a hundred grand a year. I don' get it!"

"Aren't you sick of dissecting cicadas, Ivan? It's a fricking waste of time. I've spent more than two years diddling my life away on goddamn *Arctica islandia*, a smelly quahog clam that lives in ocean mud for four or five hundred years. Three cheers for the old darling. St. James thinks there's some genetic secret code in a damn clam or a tortoise or rockfish that can be transferred to humans. Of course we might have to live at the bottom of the Arctic ocean! Maybe he'll try a Sequoia gene next – so humans can live for a couple of thousand years. We've killed a dozen rare tuataras and injected their DNA into those hapless goddam monkeys. Half the time the poor things die a terrible death. I thought we'd be working on bio-medicines. Instead we're playing God in a biological asylum. I'm getting out."

"You sure you're not just pissed about your coffee?" Ivan asked, still smiling like a chubby cherub.

"I AM pissed off about my coffee," he shouted. "Still smuggle in my pistachios, he confided. But mostly I'm just mad at myself. I was making some real progress on an enzyme that might prevent lymphoma and leukemia. St. James promised me unlimited lab resources to continue my research. Then he gives me clams. I'm going back to my little lab in Mill Valley. After work I'll order clam chowder and grilled rockfish. Good luck with your cicada project."

Ivan laughed uneasily and shook Jimmie's hand. A security guard copied the video clip and forwarded it to St. James.

29. E-mail to Paulette

One day, on tearing off some old bark, I saw two rare beetles, and seized one in each hand; then I saw a third and new kind, which I would not bear to lose, so that I popped the one which I held in my right hand into my mouth. Alas! It ejected some intensely acrid fluid, which burnt my tongue so that I was forced to spit the beetle out, which was los, as was the first one.

- Charles Darwin

Dear Paulette,

I've fallen into a routine of collecting, preserving, photographing and just observing this amazing and often bizarre place. Every day I make a discovery that thrills me — a carnivorous fungus, a plant that shoots needle-like seeds, a wasp with terrible stinging jaws and a nasty stinger. Here I am in my microdot of an ecosystem, never farther than 10 miles from my cozy little cabin, on one of the world's largest islands. I could spend a hundred lifetimes here just discovering new wonders.

I love the gentle, loving laughing people. They have so little — their rice and their proud herd of cattle, a communal flock of guinea fowl and their music, barefoot children covered with dust. But they are so damned happy, so trusting. I love them, especially the children and above all, little Raozy.

Every day I discover species new to science. It's overwhelming. Mamba is ecstatic to see the national collection growing and keeps me in kippers and my favorite tobacco as long as I supply him with weevils.

My personal collection has grown as well — I wonder where the department is storing all the boxes. Found a lovely burrowing cockroach built like a VW bug, about the size of a golf ball. And I think I've got a good candidate for the world's largest ant. Speaking of ants, take a look at the attached photo. This young boy fell onto a sharp rock and tore his thigh. See the stitches? Guess what they are? Ant heads! There's a nasty soldier ant here with fearsome jaws. The Rock People use them to suture a wound. They hold the ant next to the skin and it sinks its jaws into the skin. Then they snap off the head with a thumbnail and the head stays imbedded like a staple, closing the wound and maybe even protecting against infection! My students are going to love this photo.

I've caught a spectacular centipede, jet black and hairy with crimson legs. It's nearly a foot long. My hut's on stilts but centipedes and even the occasional scorpion finds a way to visit me. Keep my boots upside down on the bedposts — scorpions are infamous for crawling into a boot at night. Hissing cockroaches are everywhere — I've grown fond of the clowns.

Hope you aren't bored out of your mind with bug talk. But you should see the stalk-eyed flies, the spitting bugs and spiders with poisonous spikes, the lump of bird poop that starts climbing a twig — it's a camouflaged caterpillar.

I'm adjusting to my new home. I eat rice and drink my burnt rice tea. I tolerate the heat and humidity, the leeches, mosquitoes and biting flies and the constant noise of a tropical jungle. I don't even miss teaching very much. But at the end of the day my cabin is a lonely place. This may not make sense but the more I settle in, and the closer I get to my village friends, the more I miss Massachusetts. I afraid I might lose myself.

Back to bugs. The next picture is Polybothris paulettis. *Yep, you have a beetle named after you. Green, cobalt blue, red violet — it's a beauty — will go well with your emerald dress. How'd you like to wear a beetle as a pendant? Mamba and I now have the definitive collection of* Polybothris *beetles — better than the Smithsonian collection.*

Almost every Saturday morning I join a parade of villagers walking the six-mile dirt road to Beramanja. It's market day! The perfect place to buy a variety of live grubs (eaten raw or lightly roasted), toasted grasshoppers and tiny black scorpions, gunny sacks of ice, fresh fruit and yams, dark brown dried fish dotted with flies, hand-woven hats and vanilla beans. My favorite thing is the homemade paper, decorated with pressed leaves and flowers.

I had to throw away my first few sheets – they started growing mold! I'm sending you a few non-moldy ones.

I pull my little wooden wagon all the way to Beramanja piled high with boxes of bugs to send to The Chapter, to Mamba and to Harvard. On the way back I bring gifts for the village – fruit, vanilla beans and maybe a couple of live guinea hens – the eggs are wonderful and the villagers eat surprisingly little protein. The village elder smokes a wooden pipe and seems to like the horrible black tobacco I bring him – although he often smokes some kind of dry moss that hangs from the palm trees. My gifts help to pay my little army of collectors who have found hundreds of fine specimens. I have a great surprise for the village – I've bought two zebu calves. They're supposed to arrive at the next Saturday market.

The Chapter is really getting on my nerves. I'm sending them brand new species of wasps and beetles, interesting fungi and centipedes, rare flowers and bioluminescent mushrooms. All I get back is a sense of frustration, anxiety and disappointment. They want magic. A potion for eternal youth. St. James actually believes it exists. He has" instructed" me to get the secret from the village elders. Damn him!

I'm ready for a vacation. The jungle is claustrophobic. I'm tired. Thinking of visiting Mamba. It's cooler in Tana and I'm ready for a French restaurant and a bottle of wine. Hey – why not join us?

Mamba often has a package for me with wonderful treats – rich bitter Madagascar chocolate (usually melted from the heat), canned brown bread and baked beans, and – bless the man – lemon curd! Last week he sent me a magnificent gift; a huge stuffed fruit bat with a 30-inch wingspan. Think I'll hang it over my bed when I get home.

I've been to the funeral grounds of the Rock People. Each grave has a carved totem. The carvings are bizarre erotica, figures mating with animals and birds. On the top of each totem is a longhorn beetle, instead of the more traditional carved zebu horns. I'm sure it's a longhorn The Chapter expects me to find. I feel like telling St. James to try copulating with a lemur or a parrot.

Good night my spymaster. It's raining – good time to sleep – the jungle noises almost disappear when it rains.

30. Paulette answers

Dear Tryg,

How romantic, a beetle named after me. And wearing a dead beetle – little dead legs on my neck – a dream come true! I'm sure a giant bat hanging over your bed will be quite the babe magnet!

I think you've been in the jungle too long. How about you just send me the potion that will keep me young and sexy for a couple of centuries!

I'm sure St. James will love it when you tell him to fuck a parrot. Oops! Did I say that! You were much more, er, scientific and diplomatic to say "copulate."

Will think of you drinking your burnt rice tea this afternoon – I'm stopping by the local coffee shop for a caramel latte!

Be well. I miss my rookie spy.

31. Funeral

The Madagascan legends relate that the lolopaty [butterflies] *represent the spirits of the deceased who have returned to the living.*

- Paul Griveaud

The ceremony began at dusk. One of the village elders had died the previous day and Tryg knew the funeral ceremony was imminent. He had asked the villagers about the event, but they were strangely secretive. The simply answered, *"miandry sy mahita"* (wait and see). At first Tryg couldn't place the high-pitched sounds. Some new insect hatch? Distant sirens? Impossible. He stepped outside and saw them— the women of the village in the clearing, wailing, on their knees, rocking back and forth. The wailing was communal; it was song. At times the pitch and volume were low and muted, fluctuating in rhythmic waves; then, abruptly, the voices would peak in a high-pitched ululation, an intense laser-beam of piercing sound followed by a moment of dramatic silence before the ritual was repeated. Suddenly, the women stood and disappeared from the clearing. Tryg wasn't sure what was happening; he diffidently approached the village center to observe the ceremony first-hand.

Even the jungle seemed to pause—no scolding lemurs, no screaming birds—an eerie stillness. Then far-off he heard the rumbling. Drums? Was it the men's turn to wail? Where were the women? For that matter, where was anyone? The clearing was deserted, The rumbling growing louder; he actually felt the earth trembling at his feet.

Suddenly they appeared—the zebus. All the cattle owned by the Rock People were stampeding. Red dust rose in a huge cloud, obscuring the long-horned beasts as they charged and bellowed through the now-deserted village. Tryg began to wheeze and quickly took a puff of Proventil. Trailing the stampede, boys and men ran whooping and waving thin bamboo poles. The strange parade ended as abruptly as it had begun. The suffocating red dust began to dissipate in the gentle breeze. The men and boys gathered together, congratulating themselves. The cattle, apparently, were settling down, spreading across the countryside to graze.

Tryg wasn't sure if he should join his friends. He wanted to share their grief, or whatever emotions they were expressing, but didn't understand their rituals. He walked slowly to join the others who were gathering in front of the elder's hut. As he approached, he saw a fallen zebu, several arrows piercing its side. Two men straddled the dying bull and withdrew sharp knives from their belts.

Now the women and children reappeared, many carrying dry branches. In the center of the communal clearing several men were digging a pit. Near the pit, the women and children piled branches into a pyramid. A pyre for the deceased? Tryg sat nearby in the grass to watch and learn. Soon the flames began to consume the pyramid. The entire village was gathering around the bonfire. Every man, woman and child stood in a large ring around it, the youngest ones in mother's arms. Several men carried drums and guitars. Tryg stood outside the ring, but two men brought him in, saying *fianao fianakaviana* (you are family). But he still felt awkward as the villagers began dancing and singing to the music.

The dry wood burned quickly. Four men with shovels lined the pit with the glowing coals while several others dragged the bull, now gutted and missing its head and legs. Some placed wet leaves on the coals as steam hissed into the air. They quickly lay the bull in the pit and added more wet leaves. Then they gathered stones and covered the zebu. A new bonfire was kindled nearby as the dancing and singing continued into the jungle darkness.

Then came the rum. Mamba had warned Tryg about the powerful brew, sweet and fiery. Several of the village women poured amber liquid from clay pots into rolled leaves that served as small cups. Tryg knew there was no way to avoid the drinking ceremony and accepted his leaf cup with a smile. His first sip brought tears to his eyes and burned his throat. For some reason the villagers found his discomfort intensely amusing. He sipped the homemade firewater, again, as several men slapped his back in approval.

The second leaf of rum went down more smoothly. Tryg actually found himself giggling at the fire, the chanting, dancing villagers. He couldn't feel his lips and wondered what was in this strange rum besides alcohol. He watched passively as the elders carefully removed hot stones from the bed of still-glimmering coals. It was time to eat.

Beef was a great luxury, even for a village with more than a dozen cattle. The men sat together while the women brought them pieces of beef, yarrow, rice and mangoes. Only after the men had been served did the women and children have their turn.

The second bonfire blazed late into the evening. Tryg noticed drowsily that the children had left, but the adults continued to sing and dance. Gradually the revelry grew quieter as couples left the bonfire hand in hand, laughing. After awhile, some returned to dance or to fall asleep. As Tryg watched, one of the village women held her hand out to Tryg. "Oh no!" he thought. "I'm going to have to dance."

"Mandihy," she demanded.

Tryg didn't know the word, but she made it clear. Tryg struggled unsteadily to his feet and watched the young woman bounce from foot to foot. He did his best to imitate her graceful movements, aware of his awkwardness. The Rock People were obviously pleased with his efforts, grinning and shouting what seemed to be encouragement. Perhaps it was the rum. He soon got over his discomfort and began to enjoy moving around the dancing flames with his laughing partner. As they encircled the fire, Tryg saw the deceased elder, lying on a cot and covered with a silk funeral shroud. Only his face was uncovered. Tryg's dance partner guided him effortlessly to the corpse and they danced once around the bier. Then they continued their circle of the bonfire.

As they completed the circle, she took Tryg's hand firmly. "*Tonga, Dokotera*" she said. Tryg followed her as she pulled him into the darkness.

32. E-mail to Paulette

Of Madagascar I can say to naturalists that it is truly their promised land. There Nature seems to have retreated into a private sanctuary to work on models other than those she has created elsewhere. At every step one encounters the most strange and marvelous forms.

- Joseph Commerson

Tryg completed the last paragraphs of his personal computer journal entry, pipe ensconced comfortably in his teeth.

My dear spy leader,

My life in the tropics seems to be a continual revelation of irony and oxymoron. I'm living among a prodigal abundance of biota, yet individual species are often localized and rare. A naturalist should be able to relax and enjoy the show: exquisite orchids and foot-long red lilies, a thousand insect species right in my back yard, frogs as colorful as a Gauguin painting, chameleons and lemurs and hissing cockroaches. Instead of relaxing, I live with constant anxiety. In the midst of all this riotous vitality, I know that unique species are disappearing every day. Madagascar is wounded. With every rain the precious red soil bleeds into the ocean. Cry this beloved country. The relentless harvest of trees destroys unique habitats of plants and animals found nowhere else on earth. A tiny white and purple orchid lives exclusively on Mount Hiaraka. Perhaps a dozen of these plants survive. Even Kew Gardens has failed to keep a specimen alive. It's virtually impossible to recreate a complete biosphere, and many plants and animals here are so amazingly fragile that they can't be transplanted. The blue and white spotted toad faces extinction in Anpassambazimba Swamp. Who can even guess what undiscovered species quietly exit each day?

Even in my tiny isolated corner of Madagascar, the sheer abundance of species is disarmingly frail and fleeting. I feel a constant, desperate sense of urgency. The Rock People chuckle at my strange compulsive work ethic. Time has little meaning to them. One of their favorite phrases is angamba rahampitso, *"maybe tomorrow;"* but there's no time to waste. Tomorrow, another piece of land will be cleared for a new rice paddy or cashew orchard. Time and land here are subdivided into countless micro-seasons and micro-systems. Plants flourish and disappear within days, to be replaced by others. Hatches of midges or mosquitoes or flies or locusts form a sun-darkening cloud, a biomass that can literally be weighed by the ton. Days later, not a single midge is to be found. Someone with a computer might enjoy calculating the gazillions of individual midges; but take away an essential part of their lifecycle, and their annual week of glory could be silenced forever.

Last night I experienced my first wake, Malagasy style. This morning I suffered my first hangover since my undergraduate days. I joined the villagers in a procession to their sacred burial grounds and we buried a beloved elder. I'm deeply touched that my village insisted on my participation in their most sacred ceremony. Their burial ground is well hidden and fady (taboo) to strangers. The burial ceremony is much like ours, except that they wrap the body in a silk shroud. Each villager sprinkles a handful of earth into the grave. Raozy put a handful of dirt into my hand. I have come to love these simple people. As much as I miss my life at Harvard, I will find it painful to leave the Rock People.

Tryg saved the document and shut down the company's bulky laptop. Even though the sun was just beginning to set, he was already sleepy, deciding to stay home and relax. Work? *angamba rahampitso.*

He thought of the native woman who had taken him into the jungle and who lay, laughing, on the soft mossy earth. Afterwards, she had led him back to the bonfire, arm around his waist, before disappearing into the continuing dance. Tryg couldn't even remember her name. His thoughts rambled to Paulette's deep green eyes and mischievous smile.

33. Vaporizer

The aye-aye is a creature that can be described only by comparing it piecemeal with other things. It is the size of a cat, has the ears of a bat, the snout of a rat, a tail like a witch's broom, and a long knobby middle finger that would look just fine on that witch's hand. Its teeth are as tough as a beaver's and its eyes bulge out from its skull like a tree frog's.

- Natalie Angier, *The Beauty of the Beastly*

Until now, Tryg had resisted the most productive of all collecting methods—a killing mist. He hated the toxic vapor, which killed indiscriminately: insects, spiders, birds, reptiles, amphibians and mammals alike. But the method worked spectacularly well in virtually impenetrable tropical canopies. There was no other practical way to collect insects and spiders that spent their entire lifecycles 50 or 100 feet above ground. Still, he had been an outspoken critic of the machines. He had seen numbing footage of his colleagues setting up dozens of large orange plastic funnels, each three feet in diameter. The rest was simple: send the deadly vapor into the foliage and collect whatever fell from the trees. He had watched the documentary as hundreds of specimens hit the funnels with thuds. Most of them slid into plastic jars. The carnage had bothered him, yet here he was, unpacking the ominous machine.

All because a palm tree was in bloom! But not just any palm tree. The previous day, he had looked up at a commotion of screaming birds and buzzing insects. Sixty-five feet in the air, one of the suicide palms was in full flower. For some fifty years the tree had grown without ever blooming. Now the mature tree, with leaves 15 feet in diameter, had burst into its crowning achievement, a magnificent floral display resembling a six-foot white Christmas tree perched on top of the palm. Within a week the blossoms would begin to fade, producing a handful of baseball-sized seeds as the fronds slowly withered. A few months later the mighty tree would crash to the ground, already overcome with moss, lichen and vines, tunneled with insect larva, bark gnawed by lemurs and riddled by the beaks of hungry birds. With fewer than 100 of these trees known to science, odds were good that this would be the only tree to blossom this year. It might be two or three more years before another tree reached its final maturity. If he wanted to collect specimens feeding at the top, he had to act quickly.

Still, he agonized. Was it really critical to harvest the bonanza of insects swarming at the top of the rare palm? After all, he had already collected far more rarities than anyone could expect of him. Tryg lay on his back, enjoying the cool cushion of spongy moss, and focusing powerful Zeiss binoculars at the mass of white blossoms high above him. Even though he had become accustomed to the thrilling diversity of fauna, the cloud of insects and birds vying for nectar astonished him. He could clearly see luminous drops of nectar flowing slowly from each blossom like pale drops of honey. Beetles, wasps, butterflies, hummingbirds, flies and ants competed greedily for the rare feast. By tomorrow the white blossoms would start fading.

Climbing the palm was unthinkable. The 50-foot branchless trunk was a fortress of cruel barbed six-inch needles. Why were the indigenous plants so damn hostile? For a moment he contemplated simply cutting the palm down. He had no axe or saw, but his machete would be sufficient. Then he realized that felling the tree would defeat his purpose. Most of the rare insects he wanted so badly would simply fly away. He would capture only a fraction of the tantalizing new species he hoped to discover. Tryg looked once more at the fluttering activity atop the palm. Just this one time, he decided, he'd use the wicked killing machine.

As he drew closer, Tryg grimaced at the sickly, cloying stench reminiscent of overripe lilies. He patted the oversized pocket of his cargo pants to ensure he had remembered his asthma inhaler; heavy fragrances often triggering an attack. He spread several plastic sheets on the ground. Sliding the cylindrical fan out of his backpack, Tryg placed it at the base of the palm and plugged the heavy cord into the generator. He slipped on his protective mask, turned on its self-contained oxygen tank and removed the cyanide canister from a sealed metal tube. The bright orange skull and black crossbones with the ominous warning: "Caution, Deadly Cyanide Gas" almost convinced him to change his mind. Mechanically, he tugged on the starter rope. The dependable compact gasoline-powered generator began humming. Clenching his teeth with determination and fear, he slid the cyanide canister in place, pressed the "activate" button and switched on the fans. The machine did the rest.

Sickly yellow-brown smoke, used to mark the path of the vapor, mixed with the cyanide gas and spiraled into the canopy. He had chosen early morning when the air was still, although he'd now welcome a breeze to mitigate the nauseatingly sweet floral rottenness that so many insects found irresistible. According to the manual, the cyanide would retain its potency for up to ten minutes before dissipating harmlessly. Tryg had his doubts. The cyanide canister emptied in 20 seconds. Tryg shut off the fan and turned off the generator, almost startled by the silence. For a second Tryg thought it had started to rain. But the rain was insects—flies, bees and tiny moths pelting the drop cloths. Tryg quickly opened the sturdy umbrella he had packed with the machinery. The spattering quickly turned into a downpour. Large spiders fell with heavy thuds, their abdomens splitting open on impact. Butterflies fluttered spastically, wings inverted, legs tightly crossed. Then came the louder thumps of frogs, chameleons, even birds. The ground was littered with a jerking, twisting mass of dying species. His plastic sheets were undulating with thousands of black mayflies with two-inch wingspans. "Where the hell had they come from," Tryg wondered. The spattering quickly diminished to intermittent thuds. Tryg peeked out of the umbrella at the carnage. On every nearby tree branch, caught in the hanging moss or impaled on thorns, dozens of animals lay dead and dying. Birds and reptiles stared from frozen eyes, tongues lolling. He had not anticipated the deaths of so many larger animals, especially the birds; Tryg felt sick.

Crash, crash, THUD! Tryg jumped. A lump of brown fur lay at his feet. "Oh no," he cried aloud. He turned the animal over. Tryg's heart sank. An aye-aye—it just wasn't worth it. Killing a lemur was exactly the kind of collateral damage he had always decried.

Tryg picked up the lifeless animal. Even though warm-blooded and a primate, the grotesque creature evoked no sense of kinship or connection. But the rare mammal was one of the island's icons. Every lemur on the island, including the aye-aye, was strictly protected. Worst of all, he was pretty sure the aye-aye was sacred to the Rock People. He could be banished from the village, or worse. He dropped the warm, limp body at the base of the palm and surveyed the incomprehensible slaughter: a rainbow chameleon, baby still clinging to its back, three clown frogs, several species of birds. A large bright red spider caught his attention; he picked it up with a forceps—body still intact—placing it into a jar. He worked quickly, selecting only the largest or most interesting wasps and flies, butterflies and giant bumblebees. One prize was a foot-long ebony centipede with bright red legs, still jerking spasmodically in its death throes. When he pinched it with the forceps, it struck, biting the metal fiercely with an audible click as venom sprayed harmlessly into the air. Tryg had narrowly avoided an intensely painful, perhaps even lethal, bite.

Despite moving as carefully as possible, he still crushed dozens of creatures with each step. Several brightly colored songbirds evoked his deepest chagrin. Most disheartening was a small red and white bird that stared blindly with its large eyes, pupils ringed in pale blue. The three-inch red and white paradise flycatcher sported matching tail feathers nearly a foot long. He picked up the motionless body. It was warm, and soft as fur, its head drooping limply over the edge of his hand. Collectors would pay hundreds of dollars for such a prize, proud to have the rare bird stuffed and mounted in a glass case. He shook his head with self-deprecation, narrowly containing a wave of nausea as acid burned his throat. He gently placed the bird in the large pocket of his safari shirt and continued picking out the most impressive insects. He was well aware of the scientific importance of dozens of rare and new species and worked quickly, though heavy-hearted, to save them before the inevitable invasion. Already he spied a line of ants pouring onto the plastic sheets as he gathered nearly 20 different gemlike metallic beetles, turquoise weevils, several horned scarabs and a pair of seven-millimeter, bright lemon-yellow longhorns.

Then he saw it. As Wordsworth's heart leapt up beholding a field of yellow daffodils, Tryg's leapt up for beetles like this one. Stunning. Tryg knew at once he must have stumbled onto a new species. Any beetle this spectacularly painted and large would be on every collector's "must have" list. The head and thorax were deep cobalt blue, the elytra, a brilliant turquoise and the legs, ruby red. It was his most dramatic find yet. Longhorns often feed in pairs and mate on their favorite flowers. But Tryg saw only one specimen in the heap of carnage. One deft flick of his wrist and the strong but soft netting of his collecting net swept up his dying prize. He carefully removed the two-inch gem from the net, avoiding its formidable quivering mandibles and sharp needle-like projections on the thorax. Underneath, the beetle's body matched its ruby red legs. At last he had his *otensei*. He'd leave it to Mamba to identify the genus. He dropped the beetle into one of the collecting jars on his belt and eagerly looked for another as the relentless ants began streaming onto the plastic sheets like a black, wriggling shag rug.

Normally, he would have shouted out loud with glee to have captured such a spectacular prize; but the lifeless aye-aye, birds and chameleons had quelled his sense of triumph and filled him with remorse. Besides his guilt, he feared the anger of the Rock People for the death of the aye-aye. He quickly retrieved a few more specimens and shook the sheets, scattering the carnage of dead and dying animals.

In minutes, the chameleons, frogs and even the aye-aye had virtually disappeared beneath the eager army of ants, apparently immune to any lingering traces of cyanide.

34. E-mail to Mamba

My dear Crocodile, er, Mamba.

Hope you and your family— and new baby—are doing fine! Still think Tryg Mud Dauber is the better name – give my best to little shark.

Eureka! My dear friend. I have finally found a creature worthy of the name otensei. *It's a magnificent new species about 5 cm long and a rainbow of colors from red legs to turquoise elytra and a cobalt blue head. I can't even identify the genus—looks like part buprestid, and part cerambycid. I've also captured about 20 large weevils. I know they're your favorites. Several may be new species, but I have a hard time telling them apart even using your excellent digital photos.*

I caught all these and many more specimens with a cyanide vaporizer. I felt I needed the vaporizer to get specimens from a blooming suicide palm; but among the collateral damage, I killed an aye-aye. I'm devastated at killing the bizarre creature. It's a creepy looking little monster but iconic – don't want to spend the rest of my life in a Malagasy prison. It's now barely a pile of fur and bones after the foraging ants moved in, but what if the Rock People discover the remains and think I've killed a sacred ancestor? Should I find a secret place to bury the thing?

Regards,
Tryg

. . .

Greetings, Tryg, oh mighty beetle hunter.

Mama and I are sleep deprived, but baby is doing well. His name is Antsantsa, not Shark! What kind of uncle are you? His English name is Robert – no way I'm going to burden him with a name like Trygve for god's sake!

The beetle sounds like a treasure. Look forward to your photos. The specimen will have a place of honor in our museum. I accept the name with a strange mixture of pride and humility. I'm especially excited about getting the weevils.

Don't worry about the aye-aye. The Malagasy consider the aye-aye an evil spirit and we kill them whenever we can. Still, any government official would put you in jail for the rest of your life. I'm deleting this e-mail – don't mention the aye-aye in your journals.

Mamba

35. Pinprick

Tryg carefully picked up *otensei*. Freshly killed, the beetle seemed still alive, legs and antennae still fully flexible. He had decided to mount his treasure and send it to Mamba as a special gift for the national natural history museum. If he found another, he'd send it to Mamba, its namesake. Only if he found a third would he send it to The Chapter; he couldn't stand the thought of this beautiful rarity being crushed and analyzed. He picked up a number 5 insect pin, specially made for the tropics, crafted of tempered surgical steel, hardened with molybdenum, then twice-baked with black enamel. Even Madagascar's corrosive tropical climate and salt air shouldn't penetrate these pins.

Tryg lovingly picked up his treasure between the forefinger and thumb of his left hand. He aligned the pinhead on the right elytrum and pressed. The pin penetrated the wing cover but the underneath body chitin was thick and incredibly hard. He wasn't used to having trouble with longhorns; most were leathery rather hard-shelled. The metallic wood borers were often tough, bending even these pins as he tried to impale them. Worst of all the metallics were the larger varieties of genus *Sternotomis*. He had special tricks to pin these devils with their tank-like armor. He'd press the beetle against a balsa wood board, hold the pin between index finger and thumb and tap the pinhead with a tiny woodworker's hammer. If that didn't work, he'd heat a pinhead in a candle flame until glowing orange and then force the tiny firebrand through the body. But pinning this beetle now was like pushing a pin through a hard, slippery thumbnail. One pin ruined, he carefully inserted a new one through the existing hole, only to find the same spot of stubborn resistance. He pushed harder, feeling the pin bend under the strain.

Time for the balsa wood technique. Tryg placed the beetle firmly on a block of balsa, and pressed on the pin. Done. With a slight crunch the pin was through. Now all he had to do was slide the beetle up the pin and place it in the special mailing box for Mamba. As he carelessly pinched the thorax between his thumb and index finger, he was shocked by a searing jolt of pain. He had forgotten about the sharp spikes protruding from the thorax, just behind the head. Many longhorns sported such nasty weapons, and it wasn't the first time he had impaled himself. But the pain was totally unexpected. His finger, envenomed on the tiny projection, was on fire. He suddenly began gasping for air. Asthma attack, he thought, wondering where he had put his inhaler. Quickly pinning the beetle into the pristine white foamcore bottom of the mailing box, he set it in the freezer, then staggered toward the bathroom, gagging as bile burned his throat. When the room began to tilt, he realized vaguely he was in trouble. Everything was slowing down; he was losing feeling in his hands and feet. As if in slow motion, he felt his legs buckle as a flash of light exploded in his head. He didn't feel a thing as he crumpled to the ground, but heard a distant thump as his head hit the wood floor.

The world turned black.

36. Awake

He who would tamper with the vast and secret forces that animate the world may well fall a victim to them. And if the end were attained, if at last you emerged from the trial ever beautiful and ever young, defying time and evil, and lifted above the natural decay of flesh and intellect, who shall say that the awesome change would bring you happiness?

— H. Rider Haggard, *She*

Tryg heard distant shouting. The sound grew louder. Someone was running toward him, yelling. Suddenly the racket stopped; he was panting. As if a mental fog were gradually lifting, Tryg realized he must have been the one shouting. He sat up in the bathroom, disoriented, remembering the sting of his prized beetle. Vague memories teased him as he struggled to his feet, unsteady and longing desperately for water. As he downed a full glass, he glanced in the bathroom mirror and saw a shadow of scraggly beard. It looked as if he hadn't shaved for several days. But there was something else. He looked different somehow. He tried unsuccessfully to run a comb through his matted hair. A moment later he had slipped out of his clothes and stepped into the shower, his blurred vision clearing as he luxuriated in the steam and lather. Suddenly he was aware of an awful taste in his mouth and vigorously brushed his teeth.

Immensely refreshed, Tryg downed a second glass of water and looked at his watch. The date read "25"; he had been out for three days. He cleared the steam from the bathroom mirror and shaved, wincing as the razor tugged at his beard. He was now breathing more regularly and the vertigo was passing. He remembered the hellacious pinprick but saw no trace of swelling on his thumb or forefinger. He drew in a deep breath, surprised. The chronic restriction in his lungs gone. Eagerly rummaging through his medical supplies, he extracted the peak flow meter, drew in a full breath and exhaled with a powerful burst: 750 out of a max of 800. Since developing asthma, his top score had been 550. He drew another intoxicating full breath, feeling exhilarated and surging with energy.

He sprang to his feet and returned to the mirror, examining himself with increased scrutiny. His hairline . . . he was certain it was fuller. Had he lost creases near his eyes? There could be no doubt about his effortless breathing. Then his heart skipped a beat. The scar above his knee from a biking accident—gone. He looked at his other leg, not quite believing his own senses. He tried to remember when he had tumbled over the handlebars on Vail pass, lucky to have survived the accident with only a gashed leg. Must have been 10, maybe 12 years ago. But the scar had definitely disappeared.

Gradually Tryg felt an incoming wave of tumbling emotions: fear, sadness, frustration—one emotion toppling over another in confusion. He stared into the mirror. There was no doubt about it—his face was a much younger version of himself. He was overwhelmed both with the sense that he seemed to be occupying a younger, healthier, more athletic body as well as the contemplation of the consequences of his situation. He had been impaled by the very beetle The Chapter was seeking. As a living, breathing guinea pig of the fountain-of-youth beetle's sting, Tryg would instantly become a world celebrity. Worse than that, Tryg thought with genuine terror, opportunists would descend upon the Rock People to find more beetles; and Tryg could only speculate in horror about the way The Chapter would quickly identify the active molecules in *otensei* and market the drug to the ultra-wealthy.

Stunned, Tryg sat at his computer table. Elbows resting on the desk, head nestled in his hands, Tryg thought of yet more harrowing consequences of his accident. He had to protect his beloved Rock People from unprecedented intrusion, and he couldn't let The Chapter exploit and manipulate the natural longevity of humankind.

Otensei—Tryg had discovered the fountain-of-youth beetle.

37. Call for help

After sitting long in deep thought, Tryg inserted the card in his laptop which dutifully paused with a blank screen and then quickly re-opened. He double-clicked the bumble bee icon and began typing.

Paulette and Mamba,

I'm going to need your help. I've discovered the beetle The Chapter wants so desperately. No doubt at all—it's real. It's a great rarity and incredibly beautiful, but we can't let it fall into the hands of The Chapter. I'm guessing its life cycle is connected with the suicide palms that grow here and bloom only once (takes some 50 years for them to mature). Maybe there's a special enzyme in the palm's nectar. I'm sure this beetle's the real thing. It "stung" me; I was knocked out for three days. I'm not exactly a boy, but I look like I'm back in grad school again: whiter teeth, breathing without asthma, running almost effortless miles along the beach, scar on my thigh that has disappeared, lost weight, hairline has "un-receded," younger-looking face.

Frankly, my friends, I'm scared. I must destroy the beetle, and no one can ever know what really stung me. I'm going to be sending you detailed digital photos, Mamba, so you'll have a record; but please destroy even these secure pics. My story to The Chapter: I believe I was stung by a velvet ant. The pain was certainly sufficient for that speculation and I recently found a new species to send to The Chapter. At first I thought of just concealing the whole incident. But I can't forever hide my new younger body. The Chapter has been getting increasingly impatient with me and hinting that they may send one or two representatives to "assist" me. They believe the stories and desperately want the fountain-of-youth insect. As soon as someone arrives they'll notice the changes in me. I'm going to be pro-active and write St. James right away.

Of course the whole village already knows what happened to me. According to the shaman, for the next 50 or 75 years, I'm supposed to stay young. Although I can't stand the thought of becoming some kind of sideshow freak, eventually I suppose the dust will settle on my situation. But what about my dear friends, the Rock People? Yes, Mamba, we are now ny namanao *—family. At first I was afraid that thousands of carpetbaggers would descend on this area, hunting for some bug proven to exist and no longer just a legend. But now I think that once the velvet ant theory is disproved by The Chapter, there will be only a trickle of opportunists for this simple fact: among the tens of thousands of insect species here, no one knows what to look for.*

I showed the beetle to my fellow shaman. Oh yeah, I'm now a shaman of the Rock People—long story—and he immediately pinched the beetle's thoracic spines. He just smiled enigmatically, then grimaced in pain as he began transforming before my very eyes. His wrinkles disappeared. His bent back straightened. He morphed from an old man to a young one in less than an hour. It's impossible, I know. It defies the laws of physics and biology. But it happened. There can't be much of the active molecules left. I'm going to crunch my beauty with a mortar and pestle, add distilled water, filter the solution and then put the elixir in a special storage bottle. It might not be the best answer, but at least I will probably save some of the unique biochemistry. Otherwise it might simply evaporate. I hate to crush this most beautiful specimen. It's unlikely I'll ever see another. Mamba, my friend, this is your otensei, *but it will have to remain our secret. I don't even know for sure why I'm saving the beetle's remains. Maybe I'll just give the vial to the Rock People. I have a compulsive Faustian urge to preserve this beetle's remains.*

No matter what, I can't keep my circumstances a secret for long. A few days ago I was a 40-year old professor with asthma and a receding hairline. Today I'm 20-something and ready for competitive tennis. Thank god, as far as I can tell, my memory hasn't regressed. I've tested my intellectual faculties and memory: I still appreciate your gift of the red variety of T. giraffe, *Mamba. And I remember that you, Paulette, are a fisher of men. I figure you're in your early 30s. I'm probably now younger than you. Is that going to be a problem when I ask you out for dinner?*

Regards,

Tryg

. . . . . .

Tryg sent the secure e-mail and waited. He expected an immediate response, but the screen simply stared back at him. Impatient, he began heating water for a cup of rice tea. The laptop interrupted him with a high-pitched "ping." Riveted on the words that began flowing across the screen, Tryg read a message from Paulette:

My Dear Tryg,

I'm in shock. Given one wish, many people would choose to be you: young, healthy and looking forward to 50 or 75 years without changing. Maybe you'll live forever. I still can hardly believe the beetle exists and that you're living proof. Thank god you survived the sting.

Your life just got a lot more complicated . . . and dangerous. This is the kind of discovery they've been counting on and they may suspect you're hiding something. Maybe you should just come back to Harvard now under our protection.

The news from The Chapter is bad and getting worse. It has been planning to send Marvin to visit you, possibly with a Malagasy translator. Why are they sending Marvin on such an important mission, especially after the tragedy in Peru? All our evidence points to him as the murderer. Sounds like a good idea telling The Chapter about the velvet ant. After all, you were unconscious for three days. You can't be sure what stung you. The Chapter simply can't get its hands on this beetle. It will want that fountain of youth elixir in the worst way. Again, be careful of Marvin—I think he's more than dangerous. He was definitely one of the white men in Peru when the shaman was killed

Paulette, your loving spymaster

P.S., Dinner with you in Boston? It's a date.

. . .

Dear Green Eyes,

What a mess. I feel pretty confident that I can put off The Chapter. After all, I'm letting them know right away about my sting and the results. They will soon find out that I'm mistaken about the velvet ant, but there's no reason to suspect me of hiding anything. As far as Marvin is concerned, I still can hardly believe he'd kill someone, despite being utterly obnoxious and a bully. Besides, he's dumb as dirt.

However, there's no way I'm leaving and returning to Harvard. The Chapter would know I had found the fountain-of-youth beetle. I need to play this game out to its conclusion. Wish me luck. By the way, there is a scientific precedent for this youth beetle. Scientists have discovered a gene in some fruit flies that doubles its lifespan from five weeks to ten weeks. Not only does the fruit fly live twice as long, but during its extended lifespan it stays young and sexually active. If my sting works the same way, I might live an extra 50 years or more, but remain looking like a 25-year-old.

Hope I'm not too young for you.

P.S. Would you wear a beautiful beetle around your neck as a pendant?

Tryg

. . .

Mamba,

Here are the digital photos of otensei. *You should at least see your namesake before I have to destroy it. If the museum ever manages to acquire another one, I know I can count on you to find a way for it to disappear. Please destroy these digital photos. Even with all our security I'm afraid to have a visual record.*

Tryg

. . .

Hi Tryg

My dear friend, how can I help you? The Chapter certainly isn't going to like the biochemistry of the velvet ant. If they think you're lying to them your safety could be in danger. Paulette's warning about Marvin is pretty scary too. About all I can do is to look out for any specimens sent to the museum and to destroy them. Otensei appears to be an entirely new family of beetles, a longhorn metallic beetle. Too bad we have to hide such an important find, but I'll do my part. Maybe you should have named it pandorai.

Maybe Paulette's right. You could leave Madagascar right away. But if you run . . . I guess I don't have to state the obvious. I hope you're a good poker player.

Be careful. Sounds as if this Marvin is a thoroughly rotten egg.

Mamba

Tryg sat at the computer screen, lost in thought. Cascades of emotions began arranging themselves into priorities.

Pipe firmly clenched between his teeth, Tryg began formulating his own plan.

38. Tryg writes to St. James

Dear Ben,

(Tryg hoped the familiar address would rankle his benefactor). *I have some amazing news for you. A few days ago something delivered a very painful sting or bite above my ankle and I barely managed to get to the bathroom before passing out. I awoke three days later.*

I've experienced some extraordinary changes—actually grown younger. I mean, I've actually gone back in biological time. All the myths about the sting of a rare insect seem to be true. It has been so many generations since an elder has been stung that the Rock People can't even describe the insect any more. They just call it bibikely, *a generic word for any kind of insect. The first thing I noticed was that a scar above my left knee—an old biking injury—has completely disappeared. My asthma is gone too. And I have more hair! I figure I've grown something like 15 years younger.*

This is undoubtedly the kind of breakthrough discovery you hoped for. It's perhaps the Holy Grail of scientific discoveries—something that cures disease and makes us young at the same time. Of course I don't know how long this miracle will last. I may start shriveling up like some B-movie vampire struck by the rays of dawn. I may soon turn back to my original self. But I have gradually earned the trust of the tribal people here. Because I saved one of the children from a bad reaction to a wasp sting, they treat me like a shaman or elder brought here by one of their ancestors. They assure me I will stay young for a thousand moons. Their sense of time, of course, is pretty vague. But there's no doubt about my renewed youth.

The quintessential question is: what stung me? I'm pretty sure it was a rare velvet ant, actually a wingless wasp. When I woke up, I found a new species dead on the floor of my porch—about 2 cm long, hairy, like a bumble bee and deep crimson, with shiny black legs and antennae. Like a honey bee, this velvet ant must die after stinging. I crushed it with mortar and pestle and have preserved its remains in distilled water in order to save its chemistry from further evaporation. It is safely stored and refrigerated in one of the UV-filtered cobalt blue vials. Even with a few days of evaporation, there should be enough trace chemistry to identify and re-create the active molecules. My "army" of children and I are looking for another living velvet ant to send you.

Because this discovery is almost incomprehensively valuable, perhaps even dangerous, (I can only begin to imagine the bio-ethical challenges.) I'm writing for your advice on how to ensure its safe transportation. I suggest a personal courier. There is too much risk and delay with the postal arrangements here. It is certainly new to science. Mamba has seen the digital photographs. I've named it Dasmutilla diabolicus—*it's got to be a very close cousin to the North American* Dasmutilla satanis. *The pain of the sting alone justifies the* diabolicus *moniker.*

According to tribal legend, once every few generations the Rock People manage to catch a particular rare insect in a banana leaf or palm frond and bring it back to the shaman who picks it up and allows himself to be stung. Only the shaman is allowed this dubious privilege, according to fady, *their sacred taboo. After suffering terribly, the shaman may actually die. (The sting of a velvet ant is almost intolerable.* D. satanis *is called the "cow killer" in the States. It* must *be what stung me.) But if he lives, tribal lore says he will turn into a young man, be immune to all disease, and live as long as the sacred tribal baobab. The current sacred tree is a whopping 12 feet in diameter. The botanists at Kew Gardens estimate its age at 400 years, though these trees are impossible to date accurately as they have no rings. Maybe I'll live to be 400. Or maybe the tree will die tomorrow and so will I. The legend is a little unclear. But I think* D. diabolicus *is certainly the* bibikely *(insect) you've been looking for.*

Again, I recommend sending the vial by a trusted courier. I look forward to hearing from you.

Within an hour St. James himself responded.

Marvin Winter was on his way.

39. Marvin's visit

Tryg slept uneasily, anticipating Marvin's visit with excitement and dread. Sipping his morning's cup of rice tea he opened an e-mail:

Tryggie,

Just a heads up. I've landed in Antananarivo. It's quite a challenge getting to Madagascar. I've been on four different planes run by four different airlines. I'm taking a private plane from Antananarivo to Antsiranana this afternoon and first thing in the morning I'll be driving to your palatial digs. I'm renting a Land Cruiser—looks like the last 100 miles will be a dirt road. Per your request, I'm bringing your granola, smoked salmon and Stilton cheese. How you can stand the smelly stuff is beyond me. I figure I'll arrive late in the morning.

P.S. I'm thrilled by your discovery. This could be the cure my wife needs.

Marvin

Tryg smiled grimly at the computer screen. In a few hours a suspected murderer would be arriving. The whole notion of someone he knew, however peripherally, committing a murder seemed almost fantastic. Tryg disliked Marvin; now he feared him. Still, Paulette had equivocated on the shaman's death: it might well have been caused by a rival tribe. Besides, he argued to himself, The Chapter simply couldn't afford to employ someone who might put the organization at risk. And why would they trust Marvin with a mission of this magnitude if they didn't trust him implicitly? Whatever St. James's logic, Marvin was coming. Tryg felt a wave of anxious nausea. Still he found something stimulating, if ominous, about pulling the wool over The Chapter's eyes.

As Tryg well knew, at the best of times the dirt road to the village was bone-jarring, with deep ruts and overhanging branches that threatened to shatter a windshield. And it was now the rainy season—Marvin's drive was going to be a nightmare of red mud.

Tryg worked indoors that day—catching up on journal entries and his photography and trying not to be too concerned about Marvin's visit. After all, Marvin was simply a courier, collecting a small vial and returning it to The Chapter. Still, the gnawing suspicion that Marvin might be a murderer sent chills down Tryg's back. Despite the offshore bank of ominous clouds, the day passed with only intermittent light rain. It was growing dark before a red-splattered Land Cruiser pulled into the village, heralded by dozens of women and children shouting, *vahiny, vahiny!*

Marvin stepped out of the vehicle in khakis, his boots and vehicle caked with red mud. Tryg walked up to greet him.

"Made it!" Marvin called out with obvious pride, reaching for his duffel bag. "Had my doubts a couple of times. Without the winch, I don't think I could have gotten out of the mud." Then he caught sight of Tryg. "Oh my God!" It can't be! Is it really you? You look 20 years younger!"

"I hardly recognize myself when I look in the mirror. It's like I'm living in *The Twilight Zone*. I keep wondering when I wake up in the morning if I'll still be young. Come on in," Tryg answered. "Just put your boots on the porch. How about a drink?"

"I could use one, Tryg," Marvin said quickly. "But I still can't get over how you look. Are you sure you aren't a younger brother—even your own son? It's really hard to accept. The Chapter chose me to see you because I know you, and I'm still not completely sure it's you."

"I know exactly what you mean. And it brings up all kinds of questions. Can I go back to Harvard? Will I be hounded by the press?

How long will I stay young? There are more important questions, too. Come in, Marvin. We've got a lot to talk about."

They entered the cabin and Tryg opened a couple of bottles of Three Horses. "Hope this is okay," Tryg said. "It's the local beer. I ran out of gin months ago."

"A cold beer is perfect," Marvin answered. "Anything to get the taste of iodine out of my mouth. I've got a five-gallon container of water on the Land Rover—must have drunk half of it today driving in the heat. But I'll never get used to the taste. Still, iodine has got to be much better than the alternatives!"

"I get most of my drinking water from the tank on the roof—it's rainwater of course, but it's still filtered. Even with the screen on top of the tank, the water collects pollen and dust, bugs and mosquito larvae. And I'm pretty sure the lemurs pee in the tank just for fun." Tryg laughed. He was surprised how good it felt to have someone visit, even the "more than dangerous Marvin"—someone who spoke fluent English, someone from home. "Hungry?" he asked.

"Starved," Marvin exclaimed, rubbing his well-toned abdomen. "I stopped at a couple of villages. Asked for food. Got white rice and some mangoes."

"You wouldn't believe how much rice they eat," Tryg replied. "They eat rice four or five times a day. Once in awhile they add a little chicken or beef or crayfish. Surprisingly, they hardly ever eat fresh fish; they dry it, then, you guessed it, mix it in their rice. They eat manioc and fruit, peanuts and cashews, quite a few kinds of bugs and grubs—but every meal is mostly rice, and it's always white; they think brown rice is dirty."

"Well I brought you a little surprise," Marvin said. "Here's your granola and smelly cheese and two pounds of hard-smoked salmon. But check this out." Marvin was obviously pleased with himself. It was a two-pound bag of Fjord tobacco. Tryg recognized the label: *Minneapolis Tobacconers.*

"Wow. This is great. I've been out for a couple of weeks and my last order apparently was confiscated by customs. Much appreciated," Tryg said, anxious not to betray his burgeoning discomfort. On the surface he was entertaining an old college acquaintance, but inside his stomach was churning. He just wanted to see Marvin on his way. "How about some scrambled eggs and salmon?"

"Perfect," Marvin said. "We can start off with hors d'oeuvres. I've got some beef jerky in my duffle bag."

"Beef jerky and beer," Tryg exclaimed. "We're feastin' like kings. Check out a fresh-laid Madagascar egg," Tryg said, taking one from the refrigerator and holding it up. "Chickens are pretty scarce here. They mostly raise guinea fowl. They're small—takes twice as many eggs as back home, but they're delicious. Sorry no cheese, unless you'd like some of my smelly blue!"

"God, no thanks," Marvin replied. "I'll leave that to you."

As night fell, they downed a small mountain of eggs scrambled with smoked salmon and rice. Tryg knew Marvin had undergone an exhausting journey, yet Marvin attacked his supper with enthusiasm. As they ate Tryg studied his guest, again finding it difficult to believe this long-time acquaintance, admittedly obnoxious personality notwithstanding, could be a cold-blooded killer. He sized up the powerful man across the table. Fatigues somehow accentuated Marvin's barrel chest. His forearms were almost grotesquely large, with prominent bulging veins. He had been an impressive specimen in college as the star fullback, but nothing like the current massive body. "Steroids," Tryg thought. The beer bottle almost disappeared in his massive hand. Finally Tryg found a question he could ask with sincerity. "How's your wife, Marvin?"

"She's gotten worse, Tryg. Doctors don't know why she hasn't responded to some of the new medications. Her kidneys have started to shut down. They say she has a few months at most." Marvin turned away. After an awkward silence, he asked, "Do you really think this stuff will work?"

"To be honest, I don't have a clue. But you can see what it did for me. All I know is what the Rock People tell me. I was certain the story was just a myth. Only the tribal elder can use this sacred insect, whatever it is. They tell a story about an old woman who fell in love with a handsome young man in the village. She was determined to find the sacred *bibikely* and searched every day for a year. Finally she found it, caught it with her hand and got stung. Three days later she returned to the village. No one recognized her and the young man fell in love with the beautiful young stranger. But when they kissed for the first time, she turned into a stream. You can still see that stream—you drove along the side of it the last six miles of your trip.

"A few days ago I got stung by something and passed out. When I awoke I was younger. A scar on my left thigh had disappeared. My asthma is gone. But I'm not positive what stung me. I found a rare red velvet ant on the floor, a new species—it *must* be what stung me. The pain was excruciating. The problem is, the wasp—a velvet ant is actually a kind of wasp—is so rare, even the elders and the shaman can't tell me if I have the right insect. There's no one still alive in the village who has ever seen the sacred insect, much less been stung by one. Now everyone in the village is looking for another one.

"This is all that's left," Tryg continued, extracting a cobalt blue vial from the refrigerator. "If I have the right insect, The Chapter has just acquired the fountain of youth and maybe a cure-all for disease, all wrapped up in one. It's the best I could do to preserve the active proteins or molecules. I crushed the velvet ant and added distilled water. I couldn't take the chance of pinning it in a box—the active ingredients might have evaporated. Even after three days, this specimen may be useless. Water is a pretty effective solvent. I've filtered out the solids. Unless we're able to catch another specimen, this is our only source. Maybe your wife will be cured. As rare as this insect seems to be, I'm not likely to ever see another. But I've got several of the village children looking for another. The natives have hidden this secret for centuries. It's ironic that a *vahiny*, a white man, has restored their secret to them.

"I've got more concerns. There's the question of bioethics. The Rock People, for whatever reason, believe that only the village elder can use the sacred insect. But The Chapter will soon replicate whatever protein or alkaloid or molecule that has turned me into a young man. Then what? They could charge $1 million a dose and thousands of the world's wealthiest people would line up. No wonder St. James kept pestering me to find the bug.

"This little blue bottle has the world's supply of the elixir of youth. Some minute amount of active chemical is undoubtedly dissolved in here with distilled water. I'm guessing that the insect's chemical is contained in a tiny poison gland Almost all the wasp poison must have been injected into my ankle. There are about eight precious cc's of liquid in this bottle. Tomorrow morning, I'm going to give you this bottle to take back to The Chapter. This may be the miracle medical discovery of all time, but to me it's an ominous Pandora's box."

"You know, Tryg, I think you should lighten up about this elixir of yours. You should be overjoyed. This bottle might contain a cure for all disease. It might save my wife. You're a scientist, but you act as if you're afraid of science and don't trust The Chapter. We should be celebrating."

Tryg didn't need to debate the subject further. He hoped he had revealed sufficient ambivalence to give his ruse the added gloss of sincerity. Before long Marvin began to nod. Forty-five hours of travel was catching up with him. Tryg set up a new treated mosquito net over a small portable cot and they turned in for the night. Marvin, still in mud-splattered fatigues, even declined the offer of a shower. The next morning he would start the long return trip home.

Two hours later, Marvin sat up, unzipped the netting and pulled a laptop from his duffel. Even though the door to Tryg's room was closed, Marvin worked stealthily. As the machine came to life, a cerulean blue glow lit the room. The satellite communications card quickly located a signal. He slid a small scanner from his duffel bag and connected it to the laptop. Then he lifted Tryg's beer bottle by the top and ran a soft brush over the bottle. A clear set of fingerprints burst into view. He rolled the beer bottle over the scanner and pressed a button. Seconds later the computer screen flashed: POSITIVE IDENTIFICATION CONFIRMED. TRYGVE SHANE LINDSTROM. "Damn waste of time," Marvin muttered. "I could have told The Chapter it was Lindstrom."

Marvin lay back on the cot, seething with hatred for his host. Why did *Tryg* get the big bucks for his stay in Madagascar *and* have the luck to be stung by some damn magical velvet ant? St. James would make a fortune from the formula. Tryg was going to live a nice long life as a 20-year-old. And what about me? I'll get more crappy missions in some godforsaken jungles. Marvin's powerful hands tightened into clubbed fists as he fantasized strangling Tryg with his bare hands, lifting the precious tennis player off his feet and watching him squirm helplessly against a true warrior. The pleasant thought lulled him back to sleep.

Marvin rose at daybreak and made a makeshift breakfast. He had plenty of time before his flight from Antsiranana, but wanted to take no chances. Quietly he walked to the countertop refrigerator, removing the single blue bottle and wrapping it carefully before securing it in his pocket. Tryg sat up in bed as Marvin gathered his gear. They exchanged cursory goodbyes; then with the husky roar of the Land Rover engine Marvin was gone.

Tryg sighed in relief; a huge burden had been lifted. Marvin had dutifully played his role, confirming Tryg's physical transformation and securing the vial. Tryg hoped he had played his own part convincingly. An enigmatic smile crept across his face as he filled his pipe. Soon The Chapter would discover that the velvet ant was useless.

With a knot in his stomach, Tryg wondered, "Then what?"

40. Marvin returns to Miami

The powerful, stocky man in mud-splattered safari fatigues looked out of place in the first-class leather seat of British Airways. His boots were covered with red clay and he needed a shave. Marvin was bone tired and edgy. He leered at the flight attendant's cleavage as she bent to pour him another scotch.

After she left, Marvin resumed his mental struggle. Bringing back the precious elixir was his chance to get back in the good graces of St. James, who had been furious with Marvin's actions in Peru. Marvin knew he had performed his mission with skill—he was the best. He hated St. James with a seething passion. Every few minutes he felt the small jar in his fatigue jacket pocket. A syringe was safely wrapped in paper and tucked away in the lining of his green beret... The idiots in customs had been no problem. In a few hours he would land in Miami and turn over his treasure.

Or would he?

"This little bottle must be worth billions! he thought, savoring the last of his scotch. "What would someone pay for a potion that gave health and youth and long life? No one except Tryg knows how much is in this bottle. I could steal some of the formula and sell it." In the end, however, he knew he'd never get away with the theft. Still, what could The Chapter do if he tried just a few drops? Marvin made up his mind. He'd inject himself and give the rest to St. James. The Chapter could easily identify and reproduce the active molecules from what remained.

He didn't like the thought of cheating. He was a good soldier and St. James paid him well. But this was the chance of a lifetime. He looked up impatiently for the flight attendant. "Hey Sweet Cheeks," he growled. "How about another?" holding out his glass.

"Good day ladies and gentlemen, this is your captain speaking. We will be landing in Miami in 40 minutes. This would be a good time to use the rest rooms before we turn on the seat belt sign. On behalf of British Airlines we would like to thank you for flying with us." Marvin tuned out the rest of the chatty captain's message. He got up and moved his bulky body up the aisle and through the small restroom door.

Without further hesitation, he took out the blue bottle, flicked the protective orange top off the tiny syringe and filled part of the cylinder, cleared it of air and plunged the needle into his thigh through the fatigues. For a second, Marvin thought he had somehow burned himself. He even brushed his thigh instinctively. Searing pain penetrated the injection point like branding iron. Despite his military training he nearly cried out, clenching his teeth and fists.

With difficulty he stood in the small room and slipped his fatigue pants down to his knees. The pinprick had already turned bright red and an angry lump was developing. Beads of sweat broke out on his brow. The pain throbbed without mercy. Tryg had mentioned terrible pain; if only he could survive the next couple of days he'd be out of the woods. At least he was pretty certain he wasn't going to pass out. Gingerly he raised his fatigues and buckled his belt as the captain instructed the passengers to return to their seats and fasten their safety belts in preparation for landing.

Marvin lurched to his seat. He had done it! He'd soon be 25 years old. Nothing The Chapter could do about that. Maybe he'd be famous and another walking advertisement for the elixir. They'd sell small doses of the stuff for a million dollars a dose—maybe more.

As the plane began its descent, Marvin closed his eyes, clenched his teeth and fought the throbbing pain.

41. A Revelation

Hi my dear spymaster,

I gave Marvin a bogus vial: filtered crushed velvet ant. The Chapter will soon discover it's not the fountain-of-youth elixir they're seeking. But with a little luck they'll leave me and the Rock People alone. If they don't believe my story, I'm in deep trouble. Marvin seemed to believe me when I told him the Rock People no longer knew for sure exactly what insect to look for. Of course he's not the brightest button on the vest. As far as The Chapter is concerned, the bibikely *has faded into the imprecise mist of oral folklore. It's the best story I could come up with. The odds of anyone besides the Rock People finding another one of these beetles are infinitesimal. First, it's rare. Second, its habitat is apparently limited to the grove of suicide palms. Third, the "elixir factor" may be bio-active only when the beetle is feeding on a suicide palm in bloom; this season's single flowering tree has completed its cycle and is already beginning to die. And finally, even the Rock People go decades without finding one. The beetle must be close to extinction.*

The only thing I feel guilty about is giving Marvin hope that the vial may contain a cure for his dying wife. She is dying from advanced MS. Oh what a tangled web we weave.

Yours, Tryg

Tryg was washing a few dishes when the computer dinged. He had mail. The bumble bee icon was flashing but didn't respond to his double click. Then he remembered the "spy card." Properly reinserted, the card shut down the screen for a couple of seconds and then opened with an e-mail from Paulette.

My dear Tryg,

I have a complete dossier on Marvin Winter. I'm glad he left without incident. Don't believe anything he says. He has never been married. He was a Sergeant in Viet Nam and insists on being called Sergeant when he's on an overseas assignment for St. James. He was given a medical discharge from the army for what was called "over-enthusiastic combat behavior." We may never prove he killed the shaman in Peru. In fact he may be innocent. But he's always going to be my number one suspect. We're interrogating his partner who was with him in Peru, an ethno-biologist and translator named Robert Colgate, who seems terrified to say anything about Marvin.

Tryg thought a moment and then responded,

That bastard. I'm actually really relieved to hear that Marvin has no wife. Especially one with a terminal illness. Winter has been playing me for a sentimental fool. I'm surprised he pulled it off. It's hard to think of him as clever; guess I'm not the brightest button either. Under the circumstances I guess I should consider myself lucky.

I still worry about what's going to happen after The Chapter analyzes the velvet ant solution and discovers my changes came from something else. Why suspect me of lying? I've hidden the real bottle of elixir where no one could ever find it. St. James will be furious to have his flagship discovery slip through his hands, but in the end, he'll have to accept it.

Won't he?

42. Intruders

*A typical four square mile patch of rainforest will contain the
following species (not individuals)—1,500 flowering plants, 750
trees, 125 mammals, 400 birds, 100 reptiles, 60 amphibians,
250 butterflies and probably over 50,000 of insects.*

- Clive Pointing

After four hours in the nighttime jungle, Tryg was ready to go home.
He had lost count of how many consecutive days and nights he had
worked. But every day was productive and this evening's collecting
had been particularly rewarding; his killing trays were all filled with
fine specimens. Even with the lights turned off, countless insects still
buzzed around the collecting sheets. He stacked the plastic insect trays
and carefully slid them into his backpack. The last item was the efficient
portable generator, bound to the top with two short bungee cords.
After months of strenuous work he lifted the equipment with ease. He
decided impulsively to reward his labor, taking the next day off to enjoy
the beach.

Pipe comfortably positioned between his teeth, he walked effortlessly,
no longer stumbling on roots or tearing his clothing on the barbed
lianas. He even managed to duck under most of the new web strands
that reappeared moments after they had been breached. He seldom used
the flashlight now and no longer bothered to wear his headlamp. Lights
simply attracted a host of annoying intruders. Even on a moonless night
he found his way with ease.

As he approached the village, he smelled the omnipresent faint odor of dying charcoal embers and burnt rice tea. Cicadas raised a deafening pulsing roar and suddenly turned silent, only to start again by some unknown signal. As expected, the village was asleep. No one greeted him on the pathway; even the dogs were silent. His cabin was completely dark, but as he approached the porch he felt a sudden chill.

He walked up the two steps, startled by the creak, opened the screen door and entered the familiar screened porch, turning on a light. He jumped as the screen door shut with a bang. In the distance the generator began its muffled humming. Tryg glanced at his work table – nothing out of place. Camera, computer, spreading boards and pins – he didn't notice anything amiss, but his heart was racing. Why was he so jumpy? Maybe it was the two creepy translucent tan spiders he had captured tonight. Their swollen abdomens reminded him of blood blisters ready to burst.

He entered the cabin and turned on another light. He smelled something. Menthol? Then he recognized the fresh scent of insect repellent—the stuff The Chapter had provided him. Someone—someone from The Chapter?—had paid him a visit. Had Marvin returned?

He looked carefully around the small cabin—everything seemed to be in order. Before looking in his bedroom he moved through the tiny kitchen and walked out the back door. He tried to tune out the distractions of howling lemurs and night birds, the tropical smells and the white noise of waves rolling upon the beach. Then he glanced at the cellar doors and froze. The heavy stainless bar was in the open position. He always kept the doors latched. Cautiously, he lifted the doors and looked inside.

Except for the humming generator, the cellar was empty.

Half a mile from Tryg's cabin, John Pierce and Marvin Winter sat in a Jeep Wrangler. Pierce in the passenger's seat, lifted the screen of a laptop, bathing their faces in dim blue light. He produced a small camera and connected a black cable from the camera to the laptop. Soon a series of photographs began flashing across the screen. As soon as the screen flashed, "download complete." Pierce typed a few words:

Mission accomplished—took photos of everything in Lindstrom's cabin. Found nothing that seemed of special interest. Sending photos and download of Lindstrom's computer journal. Any instructions?

The two commandos waited patiently.

Well done. Stay close and wait. Keep computer in encryption mode. Downloads received.

While they waited, it began to rain.

43. Miami

St. James sat at his usual place in the darkened board room with several others, all staring at the screen. The photos of Tryg's cabin in Madagascar were certainly thorough: closet, dresser drawers, refrigerator, desk, drawer after drawer of insects, pantry . . . the pictures flicked by slowly. The last photo (#148) was a generator in an otherwise empty cellar.

"What the hell are we looking for?" grumbled one of the men at the table.

"Damned if I know," retorted St. James irritably. "But Lindstrom didn't get stung by any goddamn velvet ant. I'm sure he set Marvin up. Let's look at the photos again."

St. James was interrupted by two men who talked to him quietly for a couple of minutes and then quickly withdrew.

"Looks as if we can disregard Lindstrom's computer journals. Nothing but collecting data and a rambling diary of life in the jungle. We've found zip that's helpful about his sting and recovery. His e-mails to colleagues all mention a velvet ant sting. But I still think Lindstrom's lying.

The careful examination of photos started over. Suddenly St. James shouted, "Go back!"

It was a cabinet of supplies—spreading boards, insect pins in small envelopes, a box of microscope slides, three rows of cobalt blue vials.

"That's it," St. James said in triumph.

"What are you talking about?" asked a faceless voice.

"Count the bottles," St. James commanded.

"Ten."

"Exactly," said St. James. We sent him a dozen glass bottles with special ground glass stoppers. The glass has a special UV filter and each bottle is lined with a chemical stabilizer. Marvin brought back one bottle. That leaves eleven. Where's the missing bottle?

"Get me my laptop!" St. James demanded.

44. The Commandos

St. James typed deliberately to his commandos in Madagascar.

The computer in the Jeep Wrangler beeped once. "About bloody time," Winter said bitterly as Pierce again lifted the laptop screen.

You're looking for a little blue bottle, came the computer message. *Look at this photo—remember taking it?*

Not really, Pierce typed. *We just took pics of everything. What are they, about inch and a half tall?*

Close enough. Just find the missing bottle. Look at the ten bottles in photograph #77. Lindstrom may have hidden one of them, containing liquid contents. Probability factor eight. This bottle is mission critical, repeat, mission critical. Do whatever you have to do, but you must *get this bottle. If necessary, Lindstrom is expendable, but only after you have secured this bottle. We don't care if there is collateral damage. You have complete level Delta authorization, repeat, level Delta. Get the bottle and return to base ASAP. If you find the bottle and it's empty, e-mail me at once.*

Wilco. But we went over the doc's stuff with a fine tooth comb. I'm sure we didn't miss a bottle. Maybe he buried it. Maybe his Rock People friends have it. How sure is St. James that there even is *a bottle?*

Listen, you morons. This IS *St. James and I say it's a factor eight. That's good enough for me and it damn well better be good enough for the two of you. The professor had a dozen bottles. Now he has 10 and Winter brought back one. That leaves a very suspicious bottle unaccounted for. You fail, don't bother to come back.*

Wilco.

You're going to pay the prof a little visit. You may have to be a bit unpleasant. Good hunting.

No problem, Pierce typed. "*Winter* enjoys *being . . . unpleasant.*"

45. Trapped

Tryg, enjoying a leisurely late morning, sat on his porch sipping rice tea, sweetened with a dark local honey that tasted like brown ale. He no longer missed his daily Starbucks cappuccino and maple oat nut scone. He felt at a cultural crossroad, longing for his Cambridge home filled with books and shells, minerals and fossils, yet bonding with an entire village of Rock People. He looked forward to resuming the professorial role of teaching and to the camaraderie of academic colleagues (as much with the English and art departments as with his fellow biologists). But he'd also miss the thrill of collecting in the tropics, his endearing little army, and the mournful cooing of the indri to his mate every dawn and sunset.

Certainly he'd enjoy a bleu cheese bacon burger at the Student Union Grille. He had survived without his red Leistershire cheese, Nairn's ginger oat biscuits, smoked kippers, and Friday night's corn-clam chowder at Salty's Fish House. Memories started to emerge. The baroque concerts, covered bridges in autumn, helping students with their doctoral dissertations. He wouldn't miss the insect repellent or the land leeches, the mosquitoes and biting flies. But he also remembered Mamba's toast, "Red mud gets in your blood." It had.

"Hello, Professor."

Tryg jumped, heart pounding. On the other side of the screen door stood two white men in commando fatigues.

Tryg's attention was riveted on the man in front, pointing an automatic pistol at his face.

46. Tangled web

"Mind if I come in, Doc?" Pierce didn't bother waiting for a reply. He sat down next to Tryg and holstered his automatic. Tryg wondered how he had avoided the usual welcoming crowd of enthusiastic villagers. "You've got something. We want it. It's a little cobalt blue bottle like the ones on the shelf over there. Like the one Sergeant Winter took back to The Chapter with him. We know you have another bottle; we want it now." Tryg started to raise his hand in protest. "Shut up!" The man inserted before Tryg had a chance to speak. "Let me make this very simple. My partner and I are soldiers. We do what we're told and we get paid very well. We're going to get the bottle and leave. Our trip can be easy. Or we can be very unpleasant. I'd like you to meet my partner."

Marvin Winter stepped into view. He had a large hand firmly placed over the mouth of a little girl. Tryg's heart bolted with panic. It was his beloved Raozy. The girl's eyes were open wide with terror. He held a large black knife against her chest.

"Long time, no see, asshole, Winter snarled. "This sweet little girl was bringing you a crayfish. We figure you know her pretty well and will do about anything to keep her safe. Seems like a nice quiet village ya got here. It would be a shame to kill a lot of people, just because you want to keep a little blue bottle. Here's the difference between you and me. I'll do whatever it takes to win. Most people, like you, have a warped sense of ethics. As far as I can tell, ethics just makes people weak. You might give up your own life for something of value, but you'd never give up the life of this little girl or the villagers. How about it, Tryggie?"

Fury and fear boiled inside Tryg. He wanted to fight, but was deathly afraid for Raozy's welfare. Apparently all his subterfuge and the story he had spun for Marvin and St. James had been for naught. He had failed. He quickly weighed his choices: two armed men with a helpless hostage—there were none. Nothing was worth the death of Raozy or the villagers. What the hell did the Marvin need a knife for, he asked himself. "O.K., Marvin, you win," Lindstrom conceded, furious with his impotence.

"Sergeant!" Marvin shouted, sliding the wicked blade toward the girl's throat. "From now on, you'll call me Sergeant!" Now where's the fuckin' bottle."

"Calm down, Mar- I mean, Sergeant. I buried it. It's about half a mile from here, kind of a rough walk. I'll get it—it'll take about an hour. Can you put away the knife, please?"

"Tell you what we're going to do," Sergeant replied, ignoring Tryg. "I'll go with you. Not that we don't trust you, of course. Pierce will babysit the little girl. When we come back, he'll let the girl go. We'll disappear from your life. Simple as that. Just remember this. If you don't give me what we're looking for, I'll come back and kill every man, woman and child in this godforsaken dump. Whenever you're ready, tennis boy."

"I just need to get a shovel and a flashlight."

"It's 10 am, Tryg. What do you need a flashlight for?"

"The jungle gets pretty dark. It comes in handy. Want me to get one for you?" He silently cursed himself for trying to be helpful.

"I think I can manage," Sergeant spat sarcastically. Hurry up."

As Lindstrom put on his belt with the flashlight and small folding shovel, Sergeant watched alertly but with the calm, impenetrable confidence of someone in complete control. Lindstrom was no match for a combat-hardened soldier and certainly had no weapon. Even if he somehow could overpower these men, The Chapter might have others nearby. Defeated, Lindstrom taped his shirt sleeves and pants cuffs and put on a fresh dose of insect repellent. In a moment they left. Lindstrom said a few words in Malagasy to the girl. She nodded.

"What did you say?" Sergeant demanded, confident that Tryg would tell the truth.

"I just said, 'Be good and be quiet. I'll be back soon.' She's terrified, you know."

"Look, Tryg. We won't hurt the little girl or anyone else as long as we get what we're looking for. St. James sent us to take care of business. That's exactly what we intend to do. Now shut up and take me to the bottle. And this time it better be what The Chapter is looking for. I promise you, you don't want us coming back. Whatever game you've been playing . . . it's over. The sooner I get out of this goddamn sauna bath the better."

Tryg turned inland across the lush grassy pasture toward the jungle. A light rain began to fall. "Good!" he thought as the trail began rising steeply. Tryg navigated with sure steps and smiled broadly as he heard Sergeant slip and fall, cursing bitterly. Tryg turned around to see blood streaming from a gash in his adversary's palm.

"Turn around and keep walking!" Sergeant shouted.

Tryg obliged. Again he wondered where the villagers were. He could smell the charcoal fires, and expected to be greeted by the usual throng yelling *vazaha*. As they climbed the slippery path, the jungle began closing up, intermittent shadow giving way to increasing darkness. Tryg turned on the flashlight but Sergeant, navigating in deep shadows, kept cursing as he tripped on roots and exposed rocks. By now Tryg had made many trips to the sacred baobab. He knew how to torment his follower and began formulating a desperate plan. With an adroit sideways step, he averted a tangle of lianas. Sergeant was less fortunate, running headlong into the wicked barbs that scratched his face and tore his shirt. Tryg counted to ten before he heard the buzzing of blood-sucking flies. "Let the torments begin," he smiled grimly.

Sergeant tried to stay close to Tryg despite his frequent stumbling and cursing. Tryg knew that flies would be swarming over open wounds, keeping the blood flowing with their anti-coagulant injections that also caused intense itching. If he could find some way to stop for a few minutes, the land leeches would converge. But he was pretty sure that even if they kept moving, the scent of the commando's blood would attract at least a few, dropping from their perches and moving inexorably to Sergeant's lacerated hand.

Tryg managed to duck under most of the web strands that criss-crossed the trail. Sergeant was not so lucky, growling and waving his hands as webs stuck to his eyelids and mouth. One wild gesture ended in a scream of epithets as he struck some kind of noxious jungle plant. Tryg obediently looked straight ahead and kept walking, smiling grimly.

"Stop! Damn it! Stop" Sergeant finally called out. "Shine that light on me! Oh God! What's happening?"

Tryg turned the beam on the soldier's palm, horrified to see a jagged cut and what looked like half a dozen tiny snakes intertwined and twisting from the wound. A dozen inch-long black flies dotted the scratches on his face. "Get them off me!" he shouted. "I've got a lighter—we can burn them off!"

Tryg almost turned away with revulsion. "Those are land leeches. They have a circular mouth with barbed teeth. If you burn them they curl up and die, teeth locked in the wound. It you pull hard enough, their heads will snap off. Their teeth will stay in your flesh and turn septic. You'll get gangrene and lose your hand. Nothing we can do until we get back. I'm sorry. Hot water, alcohol, salt—they all work pretty well. Need to irritate the leeches without killing them, get them to withdraw their teeth and drop off. Sorry, I know the itching is terrible. For now, just let them feed. Whatever you do, don't slap your hand and kill them. I've got plenty of antibiotics at home. We'll get the leeches off and sterilize the wound. I think you'll be O.K. Let's take a look at your knee." The knee was worse. The cut had exposed the white bone of the kneecap and leeches were feeding hungrily. Several black flies had landed on the knee as well, lapping the blood. These pests could transmit half a dozen diseases and posed a far greater danger.

"Look!" Tryg said, pointing the bright beam of light on the trail. Emerging from the jungle on both sides of the trail, hundreds of leeches up to two inches long were moving toward them. "We need to keep moving; they can sense our body heat and smell blood from a mile away." Tryg was glad he taken the time to tape the cuffs of his pants and shirt. So far, Sergeant seemed to have attracted all the leeches. Tryg turned and started walking again down the dark trail.

Finally the men could see light ahead. The jungle canopy was opening up again. The sacred baobab was only a few hundred yards away. Sergeant had quickly learned to avoid the barbed lianas, but was limping stoically, suffering terrible pain and maddening itching in his open wounds, his right hand now useless and swollen. "It's not much farther," Tryg called back, turning off the flashlight. "I've got to ask you a question, Marvin. Sorry! Sergeant. Would you really hurt that little girl or the villagers?"

"Shut up and keep walking," Marvin responded. "I don't give a fuck about the little creeps. Hate 'em as much as the Viet Cong. I'll do whatever I have to do. Just hurry up and get that bottle. God I hate these leeches."

As dense jungle canopy gave way, the dark tunnel grew lighter. The rain had increased and the trail was now a shallow red stream. Tryg heard Marvin slip and fall with a splash, screaming searing expletives as pain jarred his injured knee and hand. Tryg looked back as Sergeant struggled to his feet, grimacing like a gargoyle. Then Tryg turned and ran, hoping his desperate plan would work. The trail was a series of sharp twists and turns and even the surefooted Tryg nearly fell twice as he stubbed his toes on hidden roots.

There it was! The huge Grandidier baobab. He ducked behind the massive tree and waited.

"Come back, you bastard!" Marvin screamed. He heard the soldier splashing and cursing. But he heard something else, even louder and more persistent. It sounded like the buzzing of a high-voltage power line.

Marvin lumbered past the tree. Tryg barely glimpsed his shadow as the trail turned sharply to the right. A second later Tryg heard a long wailing shriek "Nooooooo!" The ensuing screams were horrific, shorter, punctuated by the vilest litany of dark curses and pleading to God for mercy. Tryg forced himself to look. Marvin's ursine frame was completely ensnared in the relentless web. His powerful struggles sent waves along the huge white blanket, throwing off a spray of rain. His frenzied spasms did nothing to extricate him—only a machete or a flame could cut his bonds, stronger by weight than strands of steel. Despite his relentless kicking, the soldier's legs moved only a few inches. Tryg was glad he couldn't see the man's face. "Tryyyyyyg!" Marvin screamed as hundreds of spiders felt the vibrations and began racing to the spot. Tryg watched with horror as the giant orb weavers converged. Several had already crawled onto their victim, trying to bite through the cotton uniform. They entered his cuffs. Others swarmed over his head and hands, some crawling inside his shirt collar. Mercifully the screaming stopped. Dozens of spiders were upon him.

Tryg turned away and began to retch uncontrollably. The wave of conflicting emotions nearly paralyzed him. He was revolted, sickened and triumphant at the same time. He looked again at Sergeant's lifeless uniform, relieved he couldn't see the victim's face. Involuntarily he shuddered, visualizing a swarm of golden spiders pulsing as they fed on the lifeless corpse. He imagined the blank, staring eyes and open mouth, frozen in a final agonized scream. He felt guilty for each of the emotions yet relieved to still be alive. "Murder," he mumbled, kneeling in a dazed stupor. "No one deserves to die like that. Not even Marvin."

He forced himself to take out the shovel, opening the blade and securing it in place. As he dug, the hole filled with water. Finally he heard the sound of metal on metal. He reached into the water up to his elbow and pulled a box from the mud. Inside was the cobalt blue bottle. He slipped it into the pocket of his cargo pants and began retracing his steps.

Raozy! He was suddenly energized by fresh terror at what the other soldier might do—or was doing.

47. On the Brink

With each panicked step back to the village Tryg's fear, guilt and anger grew. He knew he must focus on little Raozy and the villagers. How could he protect them? Just give up the blue bottle? Let The Chapter win? There was no other way. Why hadn't he just destroyed the beetle? As he trudged back to the village, Tryg tortured himself with self-incrimination, worried sick about the safety of Raozy and the villagers. What would the other soldier do when he discovered his fellow commando was dead? Tryg felt nearly paralyzed with dread. "Anyone who would hold a knife to a little girl would have no scruples to get rid of me," Tryg thought, "whether or not I give him the bottle. How could I be so stupid! At least I don't think he'll harm the villagers. Or will he?" Tryg couldn't think of a reason for harming anyone else, but his anxiety grew. How could anyone figure out the sinister reach of The Chapter?

By the time he reached the edge of the village, Tryg had resolved one last desperate action. He knew he might have only minutes to live; but he'd go out with a bang rather than a whimper. As he walked across the village pasture he felt strangely calm, resigned, determined. His greatest fear was now for Raozy. He wondered again vaguely where the villagers had gone; the place felt deserted. Pierce was sitting in Tryg's chair in the enclosed porch. At least he didn't have that wicked knife pressed against the little girl who huddled in the corner, her face suddenly beaming when she saw Tryg. He put his finger to his lips so she wouldn't cry out.

"Where's Sergeant?" Pierce asked, standing and pulling out his pistol.

"He's dead," Tryg answered simply. "Spider bit him. I'll take you to him if you want."

Pierce shouted a string of expletives to no one in particular and then focused on his mission.

"You got the bottle?"

"I've got it. If you want it, you'll have to follow me about a hundred yards." Tryg started walking toward the ocean.

"Hold it right there!" Pierce called out. "What kind of game are you playing? Give me the bottle right now or I'll shoot this little girl."

"You won't shoot anyone until you get the bottle. You want it? Follow me."

Tryg walked purposefully, the soldier right behind, now brandishing the pistol and leaving the girl behind.

"I swear, you fuck with me and I'll make you and the little girl suffer for a week. Where the hell are you taking me?"

As Tryg reached the cliff he turned around, facing the soldier, pulled out the notorious blue bottle and held it over his head. He almost smiled as he saw Raozy racing from the cabin to the village. At least for now she was safe.

"Give it to me," Pierce demanded. "Or I swear I'll kill you and every person in this village." Tryg looked down at the jagged rocks. The tide was coming in rapidly. He turned around to face his adversary.

"You want it? Go get it!" Tryg answered and he flipped the precious bottle over his back.

The bottle arched high over the embankment and began falling, tumbling in slow motion, falling end over end, catching the sunlight. He fully expected a bullet to take his life. He'd tumble over the edge and that would be the end of it.

"Noooo!" Pierce screamed, panic on his face. The bottle! His entire mission! As the bottle arced, the soldier sprinted toward it and leapt off the embankment. He knew the drop was some 20 feet and that cruel rocks lay below, but nothing was more important than that damned blue bottle.

Tryg now realized his mistake. He should have hurled the bottle to the rocks instead of casually flipping it into the air. The soldier's desperate athletic leap just might work. The world moved in slow motion: tumbling bottle and diving soldier drawing closer and closer, frame by frame. The soldier made one last desperate reach, the tips of his fingers actually grazing the bottle. Then both disappeared from sight. Even above the roaring surf, Tryg heard the faint tinkle of shattering glass.

Tryg stood at the edge of the cliff, observing multiple jagged shards of blue glass scattered on the rocks. All the soldier needed was a fragment or two with a trace of the elixir; he still had a chance. They both saw the incoming wave. It was going to be close. The soldier was clambering over the rocks as the wave hit, completely engulfing him, the rocks and the bits of bottle. It was over. Even if he managed to find a sample of glass, the sea had washed away whatever precious chemical The Chapter wanted so badly. The soldier and The Chapter had failed. The elixir was gone forever.

The drenched soldier limped grimly back up the steps, surprised to see Tryg still standing at the edge of the cliff. He couldn't return to Miami. It was time to find another job. But first he had some unfinished business.

"I guess you know what's going to happen now," the soldier said, approaching his victim, raising his arm and pointing the automatic at Tryg who stared back with calm resignation.

Slowly Pierce lowered the barrel, eyes opened wide in surprise. He opened his mouth but uttered no sound. A thin line of blood appeared on his lips and trickled down his chin. Silently he fell forward with a thud as several warriors cheered. Half a dozen short arrows protruded from his back.

Raozy raced to Tryg's side and threw her arms around his waist.

48. Arrest

Several government agencies simultaneously converged on every facility of The Chapter. Interpol closed clandestine labs in Sweden, Saudi Arabia, Guatemala and the Ivory Coast. The FBI led the sweep at the Miami headquarters, escorting St. James and four of his board members away in handcuffs. The only board member who escaped apprehension had already returned to North Korea.

The National Security Agency captured virtually all the data in The Chapter's worldwide computer networks, including its impressive array of encryption equipment, satellite laptops, and offsite data backup systems. Federal agencies froze the Chapter's global bank accounts, stock holdings and investment portfolios. The FDA took over every research laboratory of The Chapter. Yellow tape crossed the entrance doors of St. James' seven homes, both corporate jets, his three-story wine cellar and the penthouse apartment of his mistress.

Despite its sophisticated intelligence-gathering capabilities, The Chapter proved to be woefully unprepared for an assault on its own data and facilities. Within hours, The Chapter was shut down and bankrupt. The media and late-night shows enjoyed a heyday for weeks. St. James was indicted on charges ranging from accessory to first-degree murder to racketeering, money-laundering to torture, income tax evasion to securities violations. Half a dozen governments lined up with their own charges and requests for deportation.

Years passed before trials began, but the painfully slow wheels of justice finally turned out conviction after conviction. With dozens of additional civil and criminal suits pending, St. James accumulated nearly 100 years of prison time.

49. Mamba's Surprise

The small cardboard box was postmarked from Nose Be to the National Museum of Natural History, Antananarivo. The first thing Mamba noticed was the folded note inside.

To whom it may concern,

On vacation, I found this incredibly beautiful beetle on the beach. You probably have many copies in your national collection but I have never seen anything like it and hope you can use it. It appears to be in perfect condition.

Regards,

John Farnsworth Wilmington Cuthbert
Chipping Camden, England

Mamba was surprised and pleased to note the careful wrapping. As he gently lifted the foil he heart skipped a beat. No doubt whatsoever; Farnsworth had found an *otensei*. Mamba held the lovely 5-centimeter specimen to the light, admiring the rainbow of colors.

Then, deliberately, he slammed a book on the beetle, crushing it into countless bits and sweeping the remains into the nearby dustbin.

50. Tryg's Surprise

Tryg spent much of the summer term mounting his Madagascar treasures into Cornell drawers in his basement. He took hundreds of photos through his microscope, planning to exhibit his abstractions some day. He stayed in touch with Mamba and wrote Paulette every day. They began seeing each other on weekends, taking turns driving the Boston-Washington D.C. trip. Tryg often walked across the Harvard campus, hand in hand with Paulette, his co-ed students tittering and speculating. The earliest tints of autumn had begun painting the giant oaks near the student union. I a week, Tryg would resume teaching.

Today they were sitting on the small living room sofa in Tryg's home. Tryg had been subdued the entire day, Paulette trying to probe his expressionless Norwegian face. Finally Tryg blurted out, "I have something to show you, er, to give you." He fumbled in his sport coat pocket and produced a small cardboard box.

Paulette managed to squeak an awkward, "Oh!" as Tryg handed it to her. She lifted the lid and stared. "What is it?" she asked. She stared at a small brown glass bottle and a tiny syringe.

"It's a drop of the elixir, in a bit of distilled water," he confessed hoarsely. "I left a small bottle with the village elder as well."

Paulette touched the gift gently as if it might shatter. "What do you want me to do with it?" she asked.

"I don't know," he admitted. "I nearly washed it down the sink a hundred times. The damn stuff nearly lost the lives of Raozy and the villagers. I don't know if it's a miracle or a curse. We don't even know if the stuff works. I might stay young for 50 years or turn back to my older self tomorrow. I want you to have it. It won't last long. Even in that bottle, it's slowly evaporating. All I know is that I may stay young while you grow old. I want to spend the rest of our lives together, but what will our lives become?"

Tryg produced a second box. "I had a great speech," he said. "Even memorized a few lines from Chaucer in Middle English to impress you. The speech will have to wait. I'm too nervous."

Paulette lifted the ring box and opened it carefully. A diamond ring sparkled in reply.

"Marry me?" Tryg asked.

"About time you asked!" she blurted, tears welling. The Victorian ring slid effortlessly over her finger. Impulsively she uncapped the syringe, drew the last drops of liquid from the bottle, pressed the plunger to void the air and injected her arm.

About the Author

Jim Nelson is retired and lives in Englewood, Colorado. This is his first novel.